ROSE
HOPE

Kirk House Publishers

ROSE HOPE

BARB GREENBERG

First Edition
Printed in the United States of America

Paperback ISBN: 978-1-959681-91-5
eBook ISBN: 978-1-959681-93-9
Hardcover ISBN: 978-1-959681-92-2
LCCN: 2025912449

Cover design and interior design by Ann Aubitz
Headshot by Laura Nitsos

Published by
    Kirk House Publishers
    1250 E 115th Street
    Burnsville, MN 55337
    612-781-2815
    Kirkhousepublishers.com
    Bulk pricing available through publisher

For Alice and Bernie

Acknowledgements

Thank you to the Women of Words and the Fine Wine Dancers. You always lift me up and help me be brave.

A special thank you to Marie and Steve Thomas, my wonderful Eau Claire contingent.

To my first readers—Laura Nitsos, Marie Thomas, Patricia Maltz, and Cynthia Holm—your thoughtful feedback improved this book more than you know. I am so very grateful.

And to Kirk House Publishers and the amazing Ann Aubitz—your patience, talent, wisdom, and warm smile helped bring this dear book into the world. Thank you.

Other Books by Barb Greenberg

The Seasons of Divorce: Insights for Women in Transition

Hope Grew Round Me

CHAPTER 1

There are no murders in this story, which doesn't mean the thought of one hadn't crossed her mind for more reasons than she could have ever imagined. There are no car chases either. Who has the time or enough insurance? The only things waiting to jump out of the dark shadows are her insecurities, which she needed to be on speaking terms with if she would ever make it out of her own darkness. And there is no wild sex. Actually, there is, just not with Rosie, at least not for a very long time, which is quite disappointing.

This past week Rosie's story has been about the broken vacuum cleaner, the colony of ants living content-edly under the refrigerator, and the aging water heater that stopped working while she was in the shower sham-pooing her hair. She could handle the vacuum and the ants, but when Ron's divorce attorney insisted he was ob-ligated to replace the old water heater, there was a prob-lem. At first he refused, then said he'd get to it when he had the time. Rosie wasn't a fan of cold showers, and after checking with her attorney, she had it replaced herself and made sure the bill was sent to him. Sometimes she was not someone to mess with; other times she was just a mess.

Sunday's story would be quite different. She couldn't imagine what she'd been thinking, RSVPing yes to a bridal shower luncheon during her divorce. To prove she was successfully maneuvering through this overwhelmingly painful time, Rosie decided to find a new outfit. It wasn't to make her feel better but to use as camouflage so she could safely blend in with the other guests while concealing the tenuous hold she had on her new reality. A good outfit is a basic tool for the social survival of many women.

In her twenties Rosie could always find the newest, hottest clothes, the style that no one was wearing yet and soon everyone would be crazy about. She learned this skill from her mother, a master shopper. Her mother was the daughter of Russian immigrants who had fled persecution and very possibly death. Struggling to start again in America, every penny was precious to them. One way they saved money was to buy their little girl shoes that were two sizes too big. Until she grew into them, one of her parents would stuff the toes with old newspapers every morning before she left for elementary school.

It's no wonder her mother grew up with a longing for great shoes and a love of the stylish outfits that went with them. It was not a frivolous pursuit. It was survival. She believed that with a winning combination of color, texture, and tasteful accessories, she would be safe. Rosie's social survival instincts had disappeared. She wouldn't know the newest style if a copy of Vogue hit her on the head and wondered if this was a sign that she was close to extinction.

The shower was Sunday. Saturday at 3:00 p.m., after procrastinating as long as possible, Rosie forced herself to drive to the Oakwood Mall, a jungle of glittering boutiques and department stores. With the promise of a small bag of Mrs. Field's cookies when she finished hunting, she attacked the Macy's sales racks and found a stylish ankle-length black skirt and matching long black jacket that covered her butt, which is always a plus when you bribe yourself with cookies. To go with it, she picked out a sleeveless lime green top and another that was bright orange, optimistically hoping that the two separate tops would make her believe that she had two new outfits instead of one. Does that ever really work?

Returning home, Rosie pulled into the driveway finishing off her second double milk chocolate-chip cookie. Licking the last of the crumbs from her fingers, she made her way inside and hung her new clothes in the bedroom closet. The lime green top looked fresh and modern next to the black skirt, but the orange and black combination looked dated and oddly familiar. What was it?

"Oh, geez," she said to Nicky, the small black kitty sleeping soundly on her pillow, curled around his toy mouse like a child with a favorite stuffed animal. He didn't move when Rosie mumbled, "These are Halloween colors. I can't believe I did that. It's going to make me look ridiculous!"

Of course, no one would even notice the Halloween connection but her. Still, that was all it took to push Rosie over the edge into yet another black hole. Or was it the same familiar black hole? It was hard for her to tell the difference anymore. After filing for divorce from Ron, she was certain that the ramifications of the smallest misstep would be disastrous for her future, and often the most insignificant things threw her into a panic.

"Okay, Rosie. Relax. Breathe, honey, breathe," she said out loud, glancing at Nicky and rationalizing that she was not really talking to herself if there was a small animal in the room.

She'd been reevaluating so many things in her life, she decided that she might as well add Halloween to the list. Rosie wondered if this constant reevaluating was one of the reasons she got frightened so easily. The ground underneath her, the foundation she thought was solid and strong, kept shifting and sometimes disappearing completely.

So what's with Halloween, anyway? she wondered. Dressing up in costumes is fun when you are young and people give you candy. Black cats are beautiful. What else?

Ah, witches. Maybe witches had gotten a bad rap. Maybe what made them so frightening was that they were role models for independent women who wouldn't follow the rules. Is that why they are portrayed with green complexions, hook noses, and hairy moles on their chins? That 's certainly one way to discredit someone. Rosie felt tremendous empathy and respect for these women, disenfranchised yet making their way. She wanted to share her story with them. They would understand. Seeing truths others did not want to acknowledge, they had retreated to the woods, to grieve, for safety, to separate from what they knew was dark. But where do they go when there are no woods to provide shelter, and how would she find them? An apartment in the city, a small drafty room above a garage, or a restored farmhouse in a neighboring county? Rosie didn't imagine there would be any at the bridal shower, so as a private nod to her recently acquired role models, she decided to wear the orange top on Sunday.

* * *

Rosie rarely wore makeup anymore since she cried most of it off but woke up knowing she'd need it for today's luncheon. Staring at the bathroom mirror, she was surprised at how the lines around her eyes had multiplied, seeming deeper and more permanent than she had remembered, and the circles under them were so dark you'd need a flashlight down there. These dark places seemed more the window to her soul than her blue eyes, now framed by a thin, sparse row of lashes that used to be so thick. It was the dark circles where the pain showed the most, and the fear, and the rage, and the terrific sadness. That was her private life, her private story, and not for others to see, so she hid them with concealer. Next came foundation, some eye color, mascara, and a touch of lipstick. She'd even taken time to curl her straight, shoulder-length hair, somehow still a golden brown, naively believing the curls would still be there by the time she arrived at the shower.

Rosie now felt ready to face the world. Well, probably not the world, but hopefully she could handle lunch with a group of women and watch a young, optimistic twenty-something bride-to-be open her presents.

Pulling out of the garage into another hot July day in Eau Claire, Rosie looked back at the house she'd lived in for over twenty years of her married life. She had cherished her role as a wife and mother. Unfortunately, her leading man didn't follow the script. That's not totally true. Ron had the script down pat. He was great with words. He projected sincerity and had a presence that, along with his expressive brown eyes, made him a natural for the stage. It didn't hurt that he was classically tall, dark, and handsome with a crooked smile that made him seem approachable.

Ron loved the spotlight and the spotlight loved him, but when Rosie discovered that he was often off stage rendezvousing in dark corners of the theater with the stage manager, the props lady, the costume designer, and random cast members, it was time for her to leave the theater and find some fresh air to breathe. She had no idea what role she'd be playing next or if people got through life without playing roles. Was that even possible? Not having the answer, Rosie put on her sunglasses and drove to the shower.

CHAPTER 2

Entering the Hilton Hotel ballroom without a curl left on her head, Rosie added her gift to the others on a table near the door. It was a lovely serving bowl the bride had registered for and didn't damage her budget too much. The room held ten round tables with seven place settings at each. Her plan, not get to the shower too early, had worked. Women were beginning to find their seats which meant any mingling and small talk would be limited, though listening to women happily chattering away did lift her spirits. That was until she wondered who might be chattering about her. Rosie imagined the woman with her hair sprayed stiffly into place, moaning, "Oh, the poor thing, she's gaining a little too much weight, don't you think?"

Her tall thin friend with the big dark eyes agreed, shaking her head and adding, "What could she possibly have been thinking, divorcing him? He's so successful." She paused. "And so handsome."

Rosie considered ducking under the nearest table until she reminded herself that it's not unusual to think people are paying more attention to you than they really are, because just like her, they are busiest thinking about themselves.

After hugging the bride-to-be, congratulating all the appropriate people, and finding her place card, Rosie made her way across the room to table six, where she said hello to a few casual acquaintances and introduced herself to those she didn't know.

She was intrigued by Liz, the dramatic-looking businesswoman with bleached blonde hair, over-tanned skin, and a slash of red lipstick on straight, narrow lips with a smile that didn't quite reach her eyes.

She was irritated by Judy who was rudely grilling the waitress about ingredients in the meal being served. Was there any peanut oil in the salad dressing? Were there any dairy products nearby, and if so, something had to be done about it *immediately*. Usually quite sympathetic with people who had food allergies, Rosie would have gladly given this woman a parsley garnish to shut her up and was quite relieved when she settled for a plate of steamed vegetables.

Then there was Diane, the well-prepared woman who opened her purse and pulled out a mini battery-operated oscillating fan looking like an oversized Pez dispenser. Everyone at the table thought it was a bit eccentric until she offered it to whoever happened to be hot flashing at the moment and needed an instant breeze to cool off. Soon it was being passed around like photos of a favorite grandchild.

Suzie, the faux new-ager, shared her heartfelt dedication to creative visualization, not because it helped her design her life, but because it was terrific for finding the perfect parking space at the mall. "But then," she sighed, "there's only so much shopping one person can do, darling."

Rosie wanted to spill something on her, grateful that after paying her bills there was still enough money left over for a bag of cookies.

Anger. She felt anger. What a thrill! Much more energizing than grief.

"So, what are you doing now, Rosie?" asked Linda, the well-meaning woman on her right.

Panicked, Rosie looked up from placing the napkin on her lap. "Well, I'm starting to paint again."

"Oh, isn't that nice. You used to be a talented artist, didn't you?"

Rosie nodded with a lump in her throat . . . *used to be.*

"Well, I'm so glad you're staying busy."

"Thanks," she answered, silently fuming. Busy? She's glad I'm staying busy? I wasn't making a choice to take up needlepoint or attend a yoga class. I'm terrified. I'm in my fifties and don't know how I'll survive. I should have been paying closer attention. Rosie wanted to feel angry again, but this woman, who didn't have a clue, was only trying to be nice. It wasn't that long ago that Rosie had been just like her, and it was her question that really hit a nerve. What *was* she going to do? Could her painting support her? Had her talent deserted her? Most frightening of all, what if she was never really talented to begin with?

The lovely strawberry chicken salad that was placed in front of her saved Rosie from falling into another dark hole. Not only was it delicious but if she kept her mouth full, she wouldn't have to talk. It turned out that wouldn't be an issue. The conversation was being monopolized by the woman on her left with dark brown hair, ivory skin, and perfectly manicured fire-engine-red nails. She was wearing a black jacket over a white silk blouse that Rosie was certain cost more than her entire wardrobe and possibly her car. In a high-pitched whiny voice she explained her recent trauma with dramatic flair.

"I was having company for dinner and had called the grocery store to make sure they had baby bok choy in stock. It was essential to the recipe I was using," she sighed. "Well, they assured me that they did." A deeper sigh. "Well, can you imagine how I felt when I went to the store and there wasn't any? I even made the stock boys go into the back and double-check." This time she stretched out her sigh like an opera singer's final note. "Well, you can't even imagine how upsetting it was. It was just terrible. My menu had to be totally redone. And at the last minute. Well, it was just terrible. Just terrible." And with a single sharp sigh, she ended her saga.

Her sighs were truly Olympic level. Rosie gave her a ten out of ten and considered searching for the elusive baby bok choy so she could offer it to this woman and tell her what she could do with it. Fortunately, she was distracted when the two hostesses announced that they were going to go around the room, asking each guest to stand up and give the bride-to-be one piece of advice on how to have an advantageous marriage. Everyone at Rosie's table gave a low moan. If that was the plan they'd be there all afternoon.

* * *

The first person to speak was the bride's eighty-five-year-old grandmother, a large woman with white hair and thick glasses. When she carefully stood, it was clear she was built to give the kind of hugs where you could disappear into the softness of her body and be comforted . . . or possibly smothered.

People have a tendency to underestimate elderly women, but they are a force to be reckoned with, and a Jewish grandmother is no exception.

"When I got married my mother gave me some wonderful advice." She paused, and Rosie couldn't help but love her when she added, "I have no idea what it was."

The advice Rosie remembered from her dear mother was not to make waves or make a big deal about things, which didn't turn out to be very helpful. Her other piece of advice was for Rosie to remember to turn on the garbage disposal before she ran the dishwasher, a tip she must have read in a magazine. Her mom mentioned it when her parents came for dinner, or when she knew Rosie and Ron were having friends over for dinner. Sometimes she mentioned it if there was a lull in their phone conversation. She said it so often that at first Rosie imagined her mom thought she was incompetent. Then she began to think it was code for "I love you," or maybe code for "I love you, even though you are not quite competent enough to work a small appliance." Now Rosie believed it was code for "I love you. Life scares me. I worry for you always and don't know how to tell you, so the only thing I can do is ask about your garbage disposal."

Luckily their table rebelled and chose one spokesperson for their group who stood up and said something Hallmark-card-generic about respect or sense of humor or forgiveness. While everyone nodded and murmured in agreement, Rosie made a quick getaway. By 3:30 p.m. she was home, in her pajamas, and curled up on the sofa under an afghan with one pillow behind her lower back and another over her stomach.

Going into the world had exhausted her. "I'm not ready," she mumbled, "I'm not ready."

She turned on the news. There was a threat of war. There was a threat of terrorism. There was another giant oil spill, the largest ecological disaster yet. A young teenage girl in another city was shot and killed when a stray bullet from a drive-by shooting went through the wall of her home while she was sitting at her dining room table doing schoolwork.

Rosie cried. Not for the child or the ocean or the destruction man was reaping on man and on this planet. Sadly, she'd become numb to those horrors. She cried because she hadn't recognized that the person she most trusted, who she laid next to in bed every night, had subtly inflicted a pain that eventually pierced her heart.

* * *

Their marriage began with such promise, like sunlight on a lake. Stepping into the sparkling water, she'd felt it gently lapping at her ankles. Admiring the beauty of the far shore, Rosie barely noticed the water slowly but steadily beginning to rise. The gentle lapping turned into waves that became stronger and more insistent. By the time she realized they were threatening to drag her under, it was almost too late.

Turning off the news and reaching for the phone, Rosie called her best friend, Lou, who had kept her from drowning. Her full name was Louisa Sweets. In junior high, everyone called her Sweet Lou—because she was.

Now a brilliant architect with her own firm, she was confident and comfortable in any situation and could change from a navy business suit and practical heels into sweatpants, an old tee shirt, and flip-flops faster than Clark Kent could turn into Superman. They say that clothes make the man, or woman, but Lou was consistently herself no matter the outfit. She had short, blonde hair, and her wise blue eyes saw more deeply than most.

She picked up after the first ring.

"It's Rosie."

"I know, honey."

"I know you know. I think I said it more to remind myself of who I am."

"I get that. How was the bridal shower?"

Rosie moaned.

"Ah, not so good, huh?"

"Nope, and I'm wallowing again and beginning to feel as if I'm suffocating."

"Oh, hon, was it that bad?"

"It was fine. I just wasn't ready."

"But you did it. Ready or not, you did it, and that's a big deal."

"I guess. You know, I think it's telling that I can't even remember my own bridal shower."

"Not to worry, and it's interesting that you bring that up, because Patty and I have talked about giving you a divorce shower. What'da think?"

"Argh. Please don't!"

"Really? Are you sure? We'd definitely make it something you'd always remember."

Oh, trust me, I'm sure."

"Well then, if not a shower, how about a divorce sprinkle?"

"The only sprinkles that interest me are on top of cupcakes and donuts."

Patty, Lou's partner for over thirty years, hollered from the kitchen, "Cupcakes and donuts it is! We'll bring them over tomorrow." Rosie had no idea how Patty heard her side of the conversation, but her hearing had always been at superhero level. If she was indeed a superhero, she would be the best dressed, her makeup would be flawless, and anyone who tried to mess with her perfectly styled hair would be in serious trouble.

"That's really not necessary," Rosie said.

"When it comes to cupcakes and donuts, we never hesitate," Patty countered.

"Aww, thanks. You two are amazing, and now that the sprinkle issue is decided, I need to vent."

"Of course, vent away."

Certain Patty was still listening, Rosie told them about the lady who remembered she *used* to be a talented artist. "That really hurt."

"Oh, hon, I can only imagine," said Lou, and Patty interjected.

"Listen to me. You are talented, amazingly so, and I'm not saying that because we're friends. Well, I am saying that because we're friends, but that's not the only reason. Rosie, your talent can't be taken away or disappear. It wasn't given to you by some magical fairy who can change her mind and snatch it back. Whether you were born with it, searched for it, or unexpectedly stumbled across it, your gift will always be part of who you are."

"Ah," Rosie sighed,

"Feel better?" Lou asked.

"I think so, yeah."

"Good!" said Patty.

After a few "I love yous," Rosie hung up. The conversation with her friends was finished, but the conversation with herself was just getting started…again. She had to admit she was hanging on by her fingernails to the belief that she was talented and wished she could grab this belief with both hands, not roughly, but lovingly, and together they could dance and play and make magic.

Then thoughts of forgiveness snuck into her mind like someone sneaking into a movie theater. She definitely wasn't ready to forgive Ron, and she'd feel like a fraud if she attempted it right now. Rosie wondered if this made her a terrible person and decided it simply made her honest—and didn't think forgiveness could be forced, though it definitely could be faked.

So, what should she do? Slink away into the night pretending nothing happened, pretending she wasn't in pain. It would be like falling down in public, and when people come to help, you say, "Oh, it's nothing, don't worry." Then you get home, and you ache and you're cut and bruised. You cry because it hurts, and you cry even more because you're scared.

CHAPTER 3

For breakfast Tuesday morning, Rosie finished off the last of the sprinkle-covered treats that Lou and Patty had brought over the day before, then spent most of the day dusting and vacuuming and, with heroic effort, even cleaned the bathrooms. Late afternoon she left early for dinner at her parents' so she'd have time to stop and walk along the Chippewa River. She loved the river, felt its power, and always wondered what stories it carried as it flowed through the city, smelling how she imagined a wild earth did before so much of it had been tamed and manicured.

After her walk, Rosie drove to her parents, whose love for each other she never doubted. They reminded her of dance partners, sometimes gliding gracefully across the floor and other times losing their balance, stumbling, and stepping on each other's toes, as if not listening to the same music. That made sense. It's not normal or healthy to always hear the same music. Yet, even in difficult times when they spun apart, they always found their way back to each other's embrace. Rosie had stopped hearing music long ago, and the person she would have returned to had disappeared.

A few years earlier, her parents decided to downsize, moving into a lovely townhouse and managing to fit all their furniture into it, which left Rosie a bit confused about their downsizing plan. She was grateful that the framed Monet print of a water lily painting was hung once again above the fireplace. Her parents said it was called Water Lily Pond Green Harmony, which seemed like way too many words. Growing up, Rosie spent hours lying on the sofa looking up at that picture, fascinated by the beauty of the light and the colors, wishing she could step into that world. She'd make up stories about the people crossing the bridge and going to a county fair or to market or to visit a friend or maybe rushing to see their true love.

That evening, before she had even rung the bell, the door was opened by her eighty-two-year-old father standing tall and straight as always. With his thick silver hair, he still looked like the college mathematics professor he had been. He was not a hugger, but there was never any doubt in Rosie's mind how much he loved her. Since she'd filed for divorce, both parents hovered just a bit more than usual, which Rosie appreciated…most of the time.

"You know I never liked him" were the first words out of his mouth.

She smiled. "Thanks, Dad. No matter how many times you say that, it's always nice to hear."

Patting her shoulder, he grinned, and together they walked into the kitchen. Since the dining room was for company, Rosie's mom had set the table in the breakfast nook for the three of them. A retired high school chemistry teacher and now in her mid-70s, she still reminded Rosie of a 1940s movie star with her high cheekbones, straight nose, and arched brows. Though her hair was thinning, her blue eyes were still intense. Rosie had not inherited her mom's passion for chemistry nor her dad's for math. Sometimes she wondered if she'd disappointed them even though they always assured her that was absolutely not the case.

After giving Rosie a quick kiss, her mother began waving the very large, very sharp knife that she'd been using to chop vegetables for their salad. "I'll kill him, that's what I'll do. I'll just kill him." Turning to Rosie's dad, she grinned. "Mitch, would you visit me in prison?"

He grinned back, "Sure, Margie, but only if I can get conjugal visits."

"Don't talk like that in front of our daughter," she insisted, laughing and blushing.

Sitting down to eat, dinner started with her mother ladling chicken soup into their bowls.

Immediately her dad complained, "There aren't enough noodles in my soup."

"Yes, there are."

"No, there aren't."

Sighing dramatically, she held the soup pot as high as she could, scooped more noodles, and slammed them into his bowl with a loud plop and a serious splash.

When it was time for the baked chicken breasts, she said, "These are from the new grocery store that just opened next to Sammie's Deli. They're so moist and delicious, and all I had to do was heat them up in the oven for half an hour."

"It was twenty minutes."

She rolled her eyes.

He reached for the Tabasco sauce.

"Your dad goes through one of those bottles a month."

"I don't do it that fast."

"Sure you do."

"No, I don't."

"Sure you do."

Dad changed the subject and began talking politics just as her mom started saying something about a neighbor.

"Be quiet, Margie," he harshly insisted. "I'm talking." She didn't respond, but her blue eyes frosted over, hard and cold, and her dad wisely left for the den to watch a *Law & Order* rerun, while her mom remained sitting at the kitchen table calmly finishing her chicken.

"Mom, Dad wasn't very respectful."

"Yes, but he's crazy about me." Her response startled Rosie, because that's what she used to think about Ron.

"Have another piece of chicken," her mom urged as both a distraction and a habit.

Insisting Rosie have another bite of anything was simply a variation on her mom's concerns about garbage disposal usage, and it was one of the few situations where it was safe for Rosie to disagree.

"No thanks."

"How about more green beans?"

"Nope."

"No green beans? How about a pickle?"

A pickle? She was off her game just a bit tonight, and Rosie could tell she was getting ready to say something not food related. Sure enough, her mom paused, took a deep breath, and looked achingly into Rosie's eyes.

"There were times when you were married that I asked myself what I could do when I saw that my daughter was disappearing. I decided to write you a letter but never sent it. I never sent it. I'm so sorry. I never sent it." Her eyes filled with tears, and she started tearing apart her paper napkin.

"Oh mom." Rosie got up and bent over her mother's chair, giving her a long hug. "It's okay, it's okay. I wasn't ready to listen to myself, let alone read what you had to say in your letter."

With a couple of deep sighs, mother and daughter composed themselves, cleared the table, and cleaned the kitchen. Soon after, Rosie left with a pat on the back from her dad, who had turned off the TV to come say goodbye, and an extra-tight hug from her mom. Walking out the door, she saw her dad put his arm around her mom's shoulders as she leaned into him.

* * *

Once home, Rosie settled on her deep green sofa. She thought about opening the living room window to inhale the fragrant smell of lilacs from the bush outside, but it was late July and there were no longer blossoms.

The house she grew up in also had a lilac bush. When she was very young, maybe six or seven, her mom would sometimes cut a few stems from it and put them in a vase of water on the dining room table, and Rosie would be so upset the next morning to see they had all died in that vase. It was a relief to learn that lilacs were perennials, and those lovely purple blossoms with their enchanting fragrance would return every spring. Thinking of her mother's words, Rosie was so grateful that she hadn't disappeared or, like lilac blossoms, was managing to reappear and determined to no longer be left in a vase to wither.

CHAPTER 4

As a young girl, Rosie was fearless. She rode her bike too fast and too far, climbed trees, and thought spiders were great and garter snakes were cool. By junior high she was no longer fearless. Her courage had disappeared, going on adventures without her, and by high school the pressure to conform was so intense, Rosie purposely did her best to disappear as well. Even then Lou had been her confidant, and even then Lou was uniquely comfortable with herself, which made Rosie wonder if that was a result of a genetic mutation. Rosie had become so focused on how to fit in with others that the thought of fitting in with herself never entered her mind. If it had, she'd have no idea how to accomplish such a thing. It would be helpful if that feeling of comfort magically wrapped around her like a warm blanket. If instead it started as a tiny seed within her determined to grow and push its way up through the rubble of her insecurities, it would be seriously challenged.

Until either of these things happened, she relied on her two classic yet highly effective maneuvers: hunching over and looking down at her desk when a teacher seemed ready to call on someone, and hunching over and staring down at the books in her arms when she walked through the halls between classes. Rosie still remembered the day when, out of the corner of her eye, she noticed one of the cute popular boys smiling at her as he passed by. It was a wonderful smile, and it was clear that he was trying to get her attention, but she didn't look up, even for him. Sometimes Rosie wondered what would have happened if she had. She wanted to believe that their connection would have been terribly romantic but knew it would have only been terrible. Rosie had very little practice saying "no" at home. She took this to mean that what she wanted didn't matter a whole heck of a lot, and it was her responsibility to make sure everyone else was happy. Not good training and potentially very dangerous for a teenage girl.

* * *

College was where Rosie believed she could reappear. When she stepped onto the campus of the University of Wisconsin at Eau Claire, it felt like a door was opening for her. She was certain this was a place where she could finally look up and, with her shoulders back, march into the world and stare it straight in the eye. She grinned as she walked past The Hill, notorious for its steep ten-minute climb to the dorms and physical education center at the top. She stood somberly at the Peace Tree that was planted as a memorial for the Kent State students who were killed and wounded by the Ohio National Guard for protesting the Vietnam War. Walking across the bridge to the Fine Arts Building her grin returned. This was where she belonged, where she would grow as an artist, and where her dream of earning a fine arts degree would become a reality. Joy burst from Rosie, filling the air around her with promise and possibilities.

* * *

The seeds of this dream were planted in the second grade when Rosie's mother surprised her with a sketch pad and an instructional book on how to draw horses. Rosie assumed she chose that particular book either because it was the only one in the store or the only one on sale, but the reason never mattered. She was hooked, practicing for hours and getting very good at drawing every part of a horse, except for their hooves. She couldn't get the hang of hooves, so her horses were always standing in tall grass.

Her mom thought it would help if she saw actual horses and arranged a visit to a local farm. Because she couldn't find a sitter for Rosie's older brother, Mark, she insisted he join them. He seriously protested until he found out they'd be stopping at the Dairy Queen on the way home.

Arriving at the farm, they piled out of the car, if a mom and two small children can be considered a pile. Mark took one look at the horses grazing in the pasture, climbed between the slats in the wooden fencing surrounding it, and proceeded to visit each horse as if it were a long-lost friend. Rosie wanted to take credit for her brother becoming a veterinarian, but she knew all the credit belonged to the Dairy Queen Dilly Bars.

Unlike her brother, Rosie stayed safely outside the fence. If a horse did walk up and reach its head over it to check her out, she instantly backed away. Studying them from a safe distance, she marveled at their expressive eyes, noticed how the light played on the curves and angles of their faces and bodies, and, of course, paid special attention to their hooves. Her mom even took pictures so once they were developed, Rosie could refer to them when drawing. She never questioned how her busy mother found time to drive to this place or how she even knew about it. Again, it didn't matter. All that mattered was that she did.

When Rosie was eager to paint as well as sketch, her mom signed her up for Saturday morning classes and made a special space for her in the basement with a card table, a chair, and two lamps. The only stipulation was that she paint with acrylics and not oils, because they'd be easier to wash off and wouldn't smell up the house.

Starting college, Rosie assumed that her parents, especially her mom, would know that her majoring in fine arts would be a no-brainer. But then she told them. She had just finished her first week of classes, and like many freshmen, was living at home. It was Sunday afternoon, and they were sitting around the kitchen table.

"Would you like some ice cream?"

"No, thanks."

"It's Rocky Road, your favorite."

"Nope."

"How about a glazed donut?"

"Mom, I'm really not hungry."

"Well, how about a Boston creme?"

Rosie weakened. "Okay, that would be nice." How many sweets did her parents have stashed away in this place, and how did she not know where they were?

Apparently, the donuts had been hiding in plain sight in a white bakery bag on the counter. As her mom was putting the donut on a plate, her dad winked at her, reached into the bag, and grabbed the glazed one. Rosie thought they'd be asking about the courses she was taking and what her professors were like, but she was wrong.

"Have you decided on a major?" her mom asked.

"Fine arts, of course."

The kitchen got very quiet. Her parents stared at her, then looked at each other, and she knew this was going to be bad.

"Rosie, honey. There's no doubt that you're a talented artist," her mom said, and her dad continued, "but supporting yourself with your art is...what's the word, Margie?"

"Well, security. It offers no security," her mom gently answered, making Rosie wonder what dreams she may have given up because someone told her they weren't secure enough.

"How about going into math or chemistry?" Rosie's dad asked. Then her parents looked at each other again and said never mind.

"You could major in political science and go on to be an attorney like so many of those majors do," her dad continued.

"I don't want to be an attorney. I want to be an artist, and you know I've had this dream since I was little."

"Dreams won't pay the bills, Rosie," he said.

"Can't you at least give me a chance to find out?"

He ignored her question, and her mom offered a compromise. "How about teaching? You could teach art."

Rosie had never rebelled and had very little experience standing up for herself. Keeping the peace at any cost were the unspoken rules she'd never questioned, though interestingly enough they never seemed to apply to her brother. She knew her parents loved her even as they smothered her with their best intentions.

She felt trapped. Instead of throwing a fit and stomping off, she found herself giving up too soon. Closing her eyes, she didn't respond for minutes that seemed like hours. When she did, her eyes filled with tears as she quietly and achingly agreed. Looking down, with shoulders hunched, and her heart breaking, she left the kitchen and dragged herself back to her room, certain an essential part of herself was missing, lost in darkness, and the door she felt was opening was closing once again. She'd let go of her dream too easily, too quickly, and couldn't hear the promise that it would return. In the kitchen, her parents stared silently at each other, praying they had done the right thing, while the Boston creme–filled donut sat uneaten on the plate.

CHAPTER 5

It wasn't long after that Rosie had her first and only "bad boy" relationship. "Could this be an act of rebellion?" she wondered. What was she thinking? Of course it was. His name was Greg. Rosie knew someone who knew someone who knew him, and introductions were made. They met at the popular Camaraderie at the end of Water St. A long oak bar ran along the right wall and booths were on the left. The walls were covered with pictures from the late 1800s and early 1900s. Always crowded, they eventually found a place to sit and each ordered a burger and fries. Since the bar didn't have Dr Pepper, Rosie asked for a Coke, and after being carded, Greg ordered a beer.

Rosie's long hair was neatly parted in the middle. She was looking good with her peasant blouse under a crocheted sweater-vest and her favorite bell-bottom jeans. Greg was looking good, too, with his blond hair curling over the top edge of a navy blue turtleneck that made her marvel at how blue his eyes were. Their conversation was surprisingly light and easy. Since he wasn't Jewish there could be no long-term relationship, and Rosie felt no pressure to be on her best behavior or make a good impression. She could relax and just be herself, which you would think would be a good enough impression for anyone, Jewish or not. Greg had graduated the previous year with an engineering degree and was working at Owen Ayres. He thought it was great that she was an artist and would be teaching and didn't particularly like horses unless a Mustang convertible counted.

They talked for over two hours and when they left the bar, Greg walked her to the '62 Chevy that had been handed down from her parents to her brother, and now to her. For a moment, they both leaned against the driver's side of the car looking up at the darkened sky. Then Greg turned to Rosie, placing his hands on the car's roof, one on each side of her head. Leaning over, he kissed her.

This was nothing like the goodnight kisses from the few accidental high school dates she'd had. With this kiss she felt herself suddenly falling as if she'd been dropped into the middle of the ocean without ever having learned to swim or to investigate what might be lurking beneath the water's surface, but who would want to investigate at a time like this? After a month of dating Greg told Rosie he loved her, and by then she knew she loved him, too. Because he was not Jewish, Rosie never told her parents that she was dating him. It would not have been acceptable and considered something to be ashamed of, not to mention be furious about, so the drama of sneaking around made things feel even more romantic. Go figure?

On the last Saturday of October, Rosie and Greg had finished raking leaves in the small backyard of the house he rented with two friends who would be gone for the day. The blue sky was cloudless, and the air was filled with the musty smell of fallen leaves being welcomed back to the earth as it whispered, "lay down and rest with me."

Everyone knows the first thing to do after you've raked leaves into a large pile is to toss aside your rakes and jump in. So they did, laughing as leaves flew into the air and returned, floating down around them like dusty and slightly crunchy stars. Catching her breath, Rosie laid down on her back with leaves as her pillow. Greg laid down beside her, reaching over and gently picking a few out of her hair. She felt like a child again, then not like a child at all when he kissed her. They rose from the yard and with leaves trailing them, walked into the house and up the stairs to his room, not willing to let go of each other for a moment.

As fall drifted into winter's chilly embrace, things began to change between Rosie and Greg, or maybe they didn't change at all, and Rosie just hadn't been paying close enough attention.

One Saturday night she and Greg were in line for tickets to see a movie. From behind them a deep voice asked, "Rosie, is that you?"

She turned, surprised to see a friend from her Educational Psychology class.

"I was just on my way to get in line with some buddies and had to stop and say hi."

"I'm so glad you did. How have you been, Tony?

"Great. And you?"

"Good. I'm good. Could you believe that midterm?!"

"Ridiculous, right?"

They both laughed, and Rosie introduced him to Greg, who smiled stiffly. Greg was quiet while Rosie and Tony spent a few more minutes catching up. As soon as he left to find his friends, Greg began to question her. "How you know him?" "How long have you known him?" "Do you see a lot of each other?" Rosie couldn't tell if he was curious or a bit jealous but didn't think much about it.

Greg began calling her more often to check in. "How are you doing?" "What have you been up to?" Rosie didn't think much about that either, considering his calls rather sweet.

There would be times sitting on the sofa at Greg's when she'd mention she couldn't get together later in the week, because she was meeting friends. His left leg would begin to jiggle, and he'd want to know why she spent so much time with them. Unfortunately, she still wasn't thinking . . . or maybe she was choosing not to think.

Before long his calls became smothering, he no longer concealed his jealousy, and it was clear that the attempts he made to keep her from seeing friends were not just casual comments. There were so many red flags she could have been in a parade or in the lot of a used car dealership, but she was in love and chose to ignore them.

One evening, as once again she was about to leave for Greg's, her dad called. He never called.

"Hi honey. How's my favorite daughter?"

"I'm your only daughter." They laughed at their old joke. "I'm fine."

"That's good to hear. Just wanted to see how you're doing."

"I'm good. Thanks. Really, Dad, thanks."

"You're welcome, sweetie." He never called her sweetie either.

How did her father know to call when he did? Sometimes there is just the "knowing," and the "how" is hidden and has to be taken on faith. It was a seemingly brief and casual conversation but in some mysterious way, it woke her up like bright morning sunlight after a dark night. In this light she saw her instincts waiting impatiently for her to pay attention to them, and though she loved Greg deeply, Rosie finally admitted to herself that if she didn't end her relationship with him now, she wouldn't be able to later.

When she arrived at his house, he opened the door, grabbed her roughly by the arm, and pulled her to the sofa. Rosie was certain he'd sensed what she was there to say, and they sat with this painful realization between them.

"I can't see you anymore," she repeated over and over with tears in her eyes.

"I can't make it without you," Greg argued over and over. His leg jiggled violently, his eyes turned from blue to steel, and Rosie felt his hot anger. It was another twenty minutes of back and forth until they were both emotionally drained. His leg stopped jiggling, the steel in his eyes melted, and his anger dissolved. It was over. Reluctantly, he walked her to the door and after a final lingering embrace, she left.

Rosie grieved the end of their relationship, for even dangerous love is hard to let go of. The fear of being alone when you don't even have yourself is a very dark place. But, where did Rosie's self go, and had she even realized it was missing? Was it waving its arms and shouting, "I'm over here, I'm over here," or because it was not safe to be seen, had it chosen to stay hidden? It wasn't until much later that she realized how dangerous and terrifying her situation could have become and was certain her dad's phone call had saved her life.

CHAPTER 6

Winter had finally been kicked to the curb, and it was a sweatshirt-only day in Eau Claire. Lou and Rosie met at Embers, their favorite restaurant. Before opening their menus, Lou asked, "Are you thinking the same thing I am?"

"I think so," Rosie answered.

Their usual waitress came to their booth, setting down two glasses of water. "I haven't seen either of you in a while. Do you want to order your regular?"

"How did you know?"

She winked at them. "Two Emberger Royals with extra Emberger sauce, fries, and two chocolate malts."

"Yep!" they answered. Their waitress winked again, picked up the two unopened menus, and left to place their order.

"So, how're your classes?" Rosie asked. "Is the school of architecture as difficult as they say?"

"It's pretty tough, but I love it, and I'm sure glad finals are over. When I graduate next June, my plan is to apprentice for a couple of years and then open my own firm."

"That's a fabulous plan, and you're finally going to be able to build things."

"I am, and I consider it payback for the 'boys only' shop classes they never let girls take in high school." They both grinned. "Speaking of classes, how're you doing?" Lou asked.

"You know, I'm going to like teaching. There's a lot more to it than I realized."

"You'll be great. Molding young minds."

"Ha! We'll see. It'd be wonderful if I could encourage students to trust their intuition and not judge themselves or others but don't know how much I'd have to offer considering I'm still trying to figure that out myself."

"Well, that could be part of your lesson plan. Be patient. This may take a long time!" They both laughed.

"Speaking of time, have you had time to paint?"

Rosie's laughter faded, and she shook her head. "I've been too busy."

"Do you miss it?"

"More than I can say."

Their order arrived, and the conversation stopped as they inhaled their lunch.

"Ooohhhh."

"Aaahhh."

"Ummm."

Coming up for air, Rosie was wiping Emberger sauce off her chin while Lou was wiping it off her fingers when they were startled by a deep voice. "Hey, Louisa. How are you?"

Looking up, there he was, wearing a UW-EC sweat-shirt and faded jeans, with dark hair, eyes the color of chocolate, and lashes a girl could only dream of. He seemed almost as yummy as an Emberger with extra sauce.

"Oh, hi," Lou said, "I'm fine, how about you?"

"I'm good. Hope I'm not interrupting."

As Lou was saying, "Not at all," he was focusing his dazzling smile on Rosie.

"Hi, I'm Ron."

"I'm Rosie," she squeaked, worried that there still might be some Emberger sauce on her face.

"Well, Rosie, it's nice to meet you."

"Nice to meet you, too." This time there was no squeaking, just a little stammering.

Lou explained to Rosie that she and Ron had met in a business class, but Rosie barely heard her as she was try-ing to limit how far her jaw was dropping open.

"Well, better get going. I'm late for a meeting at a table in the back on how to achieve world peace," he laughed, looking at Rosie a beat or two longer than necessary before walking away.

After giving Rosie a moment to close her mouth, Lou asked, "Does his name ring a bell for you?"

Rosie shook her head no.

"Eau Claire Memorial High School basketball team? Made it to state playoffs for quite a few years?"

"Nope, no bells."

"Really?"

"Ya. I never pay much attention to stuff like that."

"Well, obviously!" Lou laughed. "Anyway, he was the team's star, and I have a feeling he's going to ask me for your number. If he does, are you okay with me giving it to him?"

"Ah, uh-huh, sure, okay," Rosie answered.

"Even without the basketball reference, you're a bit smitten, aren't you?"

"Is it that obvious?"

"It sure is. Just be careful, I have a feeling he's not who he seems to be."

"Greg sure wasn't who he seemed to be," she said, returning to earth, "and I'll do my best not to make that mistake again." Taking a breath, she changed the subject. "How about you? Tell me what's the latest with you and Patty."

"Things are great. When I'm with her, I can't stop smiling. We're thinking of getting an apartment together."

"Oh, that's wonderful."

"It is, and it isn't. There are people who don't think it's wonderful, and it's hard to know when it's safe or not safe to be who we are."

"I'm so sorry."

"Me too. My parents are very supportive that we're together, but Patty's are struggling. We've taken time to sit with them and let them share how they feel and simply listen without interrupting, which I've got to say, can be quite a challenge. After they've said all they wanted and needed to, we share how we feel without trying to convince them of anything. It's harder than it sounds, but who knew that not arguing could create change. It's slow but it's happening." With the smile back in her voice, she announced, "Time to go. Meanwhile, remember what I said. Be careful."

"I will," Rosie declared.

Well, she wasn't.

CHAPTER 7

Ron seemed nothing like Greg, and he was a nice Jewish boy—her parents would be so happy. On their first date, he took her to dinner at Jimmy Woo's Pagoda Restaurant, named, of course, for the pagoda on the roof. She was looking good in her patterned mini-skirt, and he was looking good because he just did. As much as she had drooled over him when they were introduced, she never quite trusted good looks, knowing they were not the measure of a man, or of anyone. So even though he was Jewish, she wasn't interested in being on her best behavior. She was more curious about what was behind his handsome mask.

"What are you in the mood for, Rosie?" Ron asked when they were settled at their table, looking at menus.

"Hummm. Let me see. Ah, the cashew chicken looks great and is always a favorite of mine."

"How about the beef and pea pods. I think you'll really like those."

"Okay, I'll give them a try," she answered, not thinking there was anything sinister about this suggestion or anything lacking in her that she so easily agreed. Years later she wondered if it had been a test.

During dinner he told her that since junior high he'd been working part time at his dad's plumbing supply company. Now that his parents decided to retire to Florida, his dad would be passing it on to him, so he got a business degree hoping it would help.

She told him about her parents' attempt to downsize and her decision to become an art teacher while still searching for time to paint, which was her passion.

He told her he was an only child. She told him about her big brother.

They talked briefly about religion. He said that when he wanted to learn more about his Jewish heritage, he asked his mother to teach him how to play mahjong. She said that she rarely went to synagogue.

He told her about playing basketball and how he loved finding the weaknesses in the opposing team and creating strategies to exploit them. He loved the sound of the ball swishing through the hoop, the cheers from the crowd, and of course winning, and that he still played in pickup games with former teammates and friends.

She told him that she loved how colors, brush strokes, technique, and imagination, along with a sprinkling of inspiration, all collaborate in the creative process. "It's often a blend of knowing what you're doing and having no idea what you're doing, and yet somehow…"

Ron interrupted with, "So how do you like the beef and pea pods?"

* * *

The waiter left their bill with instructions to pay the cashier and pointed to a woman seated at a counter near the front door. Ron wrote her a check, and when she asked for his license, he answered, "Do you need the number?"

"Yes. I just need to write it on the check."

"Well, I can give that to you. It's 456893789."

They walked out of the restaurant, and Rosie said, "Wow, I'm impressed. You memorized your license number."

"Nah, I just made it up."

"What? Really? Would you like me to wait with you until the police arrive and take you into custody? I'll gladly visit you in the slammer."

Ron laughed as they locked arms and raced down the block to his car. There was definitely mischief in those chocolate eyes, and it never entered Rosie's mind that mischief might one day turn into scheming or what would happen if it did.

Getting into his car, Ron shared that he needed to pick up a few things, because he and his roommate were low on groceries, and Rosie agreed to go with him. Once in the store, he grabbed a grocery cart, headed directly to the produce section, pulled a few green grapes from their stems, and popped them into his mouth.

"Ron. Stop it. That's stealing."

"No it's not," he grinned and snatched a small plum, ate it, and dropped the pit into the trash can at the end of the aisle with a little boy smirk. Before she could react, he abandoned the cart and rushed away. Left to push it herself, Rosie chased after him, discovering Ron at the far end of the paper products aisle. He surprised her by launching a packaged roll of paper towels into the grocery cart as if he was reliving his glory days, scoring for his basketball team. He did the same with the toilet paper, and in the next aisle it was a bag of pasta.

This was not how you are supposed to act in a grocery store, but it sure was fun. Except for the produce aisle, which Rosie assumed was left over "high school prank syndrome." He wasn't following grocery store rules of decorum, and to Rosie it felt refreshing. She had always worked so hard to follow rules and color inside the lines, but Ron didn't seem to notice the lines, or if he did, he must not have thought they applied to him. Who was this person, anyway? she wondered. Where did he come from? He seemed to feel no guilt about his behavior, which made her question if he was really Jewish. Still, she thought, sometimes coloring outside the lines could be a good thing and might save her one day. It was exhilarating to think of stepping over the invisible lines that had surrounded her as long as she could remember. Even so, Rosie felt like she was shopping with a toddler. Were his actions clues? You bet. Did she ignore them? Of course. Over their years together, when she couldn't ignore them, did she make excuses for them? Absolutely. Still, this was their first date. It never occurred to her to look for clues, and when he asked her out again, she said yes, and so began their history together.

* * *

Disco was the latest craze and Shenanigan's, with its big disco floor, was the place to be. The first time they went was so much fun that they began inviting friends, usually his, to join them. For calmer evenings, they'd go to the Hollywood Theater to see the latest movie, again with friends, usually his. On quiet weekend afternoons, they'd often walk together along the Chippewa River, talking about politics, parents, school, work, and sometimes simply connecting in silence. When Ron told Rosie about the pressure he felt taking over his dad's business, she asked, "Is this something you really want to do?"

"You bet. Of course. I have big plans to grow the business, not only to make my dad proud, but it will be awesome to prove I'm not just a success on the basketball court."

"You don't have to prove anything to anyone, especially to me."

"I know," he said and took her hand, looking at her as if she was a precious gift.

Smiling, Rosie looked up at him. He put on a show of being so confident and sure of himself, but to Rosie, this seemed like a wall, a shield, something to hide behind.

When she told Ron that she often doubted herself, he was quick to reassure her that she was amazing.

Rosie wasn't interested in, or planning on, falling in love with Ron, but something changed. It wasn't like the passion of falling into a deep ocean that she felt with Greg. She decided there must be a mysterious secret ingredient unique to each couple that pulls them together and has nothing to do with birds chirping, flowers blooming, or rainbows.

Ron proposed to Rosie in the fall of the following year. They were sitting on a bench in the shade of a stately maple tree in Carson Park. He nervously asked, and she breathlessly answered. There was lots of smooching and hugging and laughter. Nature seemed to be congratulating them as a soft breeze blew through tree branches encouraging their gold leaves to release and float through the air like super-sized confetti.

CHAPTER 8

Their joyous wedding was the following summer. For their honeymoon, Rosie and Ron drove to Wisconsin's Door County, spending five days on the peninsula that rests in Lake Michigan, just east of Green Bay. The shorelines, the parks, the surrounding wilderness, were all stunningly beautiful. In the town of Fish Creek, they stayed at the White Gull Inn, except for a single night in Ellison Bay near the tip of the peninsula. Newport State Park was located there, and at night there was such total darkness that they were able to clearly see the Milky Way and gaze at thousands of stars. Ah, so many wishes waiting to come true.

They rested on the beaches, explored many charming small towns, and visited local art galleries. Never having been to a fish boil, they decided to give one a try. The fish were freshly caught, there was lots of melted butter involved, and the dessert was warm, homemade cherry pie. Yum!

On their last afternoon on the peninsula, they drove to Sturgeon Bay where a boat rental place had jet skis available. They were a new phenomenon, and Ron desperately wanted to take one out on the water.

Rosie took one look at them and adamantly shook her head no. "You go. I'll hang out here. There's an ice cream place nearby."

"Oh, come on. It'll be fun, and I don't want to go without you. Where's your spirit of adventure?"

"What are you talking about? I have a spirit of adventure. I married you, didn't I?"

Ron laughed, "Good point."

"But, it's our honeymoon, so I'll go with you. There is only one condition. If I start to feel uncomfortable for any reason, including that my swimsuit is riding up my butt, you'll drop me back at the dock and continue your ski adventure on your own. Deal?"

"Deal!"

After Ron signed the agreement and paid the fee, they were each given a life vest. Before they climbed on the jet ski, one of the staff showed Ron how to drive the machine. Good idea. Then they were off. After a short case of nerves, Rosie was delighted by the speed, the wind, the sprays of water. That was until Ron pushed the jet ski to go faster and faster and started making turns tighter and tighter.

She leaned forward so her mouth was next to his ear. "It's time to take me back. I've had enough."

He didn't.

She screamed into his ear, "Ron, take me back NOW!"

He didn't and instead drove further out into the bay. "Rosie smacked him on his back and screamed again, "What are you doing!"

When it was clear that her rage made no impact, she stopped yelling and used her remaining strength to hold on.

Ron kept them out on the water for fifteen more minutes, which seemed like hours to Rosie. When they finally returned to the dock, she vaulted off the jet ski on shaky legs, which wasn't an easy thing to do. She ripped off her life vest and threw it at Ron. It flopped wetly on the deck in front of him. She should have aimed a little higher.

Puzzled, he asked, "What's wrong with you?"

"Are you serious? What do you mean what's wrong with me? We had a deal. Didn't you hear me screaming?"

"Geez, Rosie." He looked at her, confused. "You were safe. It was just an extra fifteen minutes."

"That's not the point. We had a deal."

Ron shook his head. "Why are you overreacting like this?"

Rosie wanted to storm away, but there was nowhere to go except back to the car, where, shivering, she grabbed a towel to dry herself off.

Still shaking his head, Ron followed her. "I don't understand. What's wrong with you?"

And so it began. Hearing those questions often enough over their years together, she eventually did start to wonder if she was overreacting and if something was wrong with her.

They were both silent on the car ride back to the inn, but the argument wasn't over. Back in their room, they squared off again. Ron apologized profusely, telling Rosie how sorry he was and how much he loved her. Rosie calmed down, telling Ron she loved him, too. They'd weathered their first married couple fight and congratulated themselves with a shower, but not together. Rosie was not that calmed down. Afterward, they took a last stroll through Fish Creek, had a relaxing dinner at the White Gull Inn, and watched the evening sun slowly sink into the water.

* * *

Back in Eau Claire, Rosie and Ron drove directly to their new one-bedroom apartment and, except for a TV and a new bed, they expected to find empty space with lots of boxes filled with everything they were bringing with them to their first home as a couple. People talked about how they'd be starting a new life together, but when Rosie thought about all at those boxes, she wondered how new it could be if the rest of their lives was coming with them.

Ron's parents had returned to Florida, so Rosie's mom, as well as Lou and Patty, arrived hours before the married couple. Together they unpacked all the boxes, putting things where they thought they needed to be put, and arranged Lou and Patty's thrift store furniture finds. Then they headed out to get groceries, returning to stock the refrigerator and a few shelves and had twenty minutes to spare before they heard a key in the door.

With no boxes in sight, the newlyweds thought they'd entered the wrong apartment, until the cheering began. After the welcoming settled down, they looked around, stunned. There was a sofa and chair to sit on, a small round table to eat at, two slightly scratched dressers in the bedroom, and as a bonus, there was even a bookcase. Rosie teared up, and Ron shook his head.

"There's plenty of food in the fridge," said Rosie's mom.

"And in the cupboards on the left," added Lou.

"We're all exhausted, so we're leaving now," declared Patty.

"Love you," they all chimed before dragging themselves out the door. In shock, the couple sat on their unexpected sofa, staring into space.

That evening Rosie and Ron curled up under the bedcovers to watch a movie. It wasn't too long before the two romantic leads on the TV were rolling over and over in bed as they made passionate love. Ron turned to Rosie. "What'da think?" She grinned, and they tried to do the same thing but got tangled in the sheets. Ron's elbow kept knocking Rosie in the chin, her hair got stuck under his arm, and they couldn't stop laughing as they fell off the bed.

The next day Ron left for an early morning meeting, while Rosie slept in. After a good night's sleep and a cup of coffee, she was ready to put some pictures on the empty walls. She started with a framed watercolor of the Door County shoreline they'd purchased on their honeymoon. Looking critically at the space over the sofa, she squinted a bit, nodded to herself, and pounded in a picture hook just as Ron walked through the door.

Appalled, he shouted, "Rosie, that's not how you hang a picture!"

Digging through the bottom kitchen drawer, he found a tape measure and marched back into the living room to measure everything he possibly could from the ceiling to the back of the sofa, from one end of the wall to the other, and this was a man who didn't like to follow rules. When all his measuring took him to the exact spot where Rosie had just hammered in her nail, he tossed the measuring tape down and stomped away.

"Ron, why are you so upset?"

"I'm not upset."

"Sure seems like it."

"What're you talking about? You're just being too sensitive."

A small buzzing sound went off in Rosie's head like a faint alarm clock, but she quickly hit the snooze. She assumed his outburst was the result of pressures associated with the process of taking over his father's business, and her heart went out to him.

By the end of September the company was officially his, and the following September, after Rosie had graduated in June, she began teaching art to seventh- and eighth-graders, certain she was learning more from them than they were from her, but not necessarily about art.

CHAPTER 9

Over the next three years, the business grew substantially. She and Ron were able to move into a lovely house in the new development near the Oakwood Mall. It was a charming neighborhood where people walked their dogs, pushed babies in strollers, and always stopped to visit for a minute. There was a gracious maple tree thick with summer leaves in the front yard and a large lilac bush under the front window, and in the back were two young evergreens. They now had three bedrooms, the largest of which became theirs. Rosie, able to stop teaching and concentrate on her art, chose one of the two smaller bedrooms for her home studio, while the remaining one became home to a new set of unopened boxes.

It was in this house that Rosie and Ron delighted in dreaming of their future together and six months later were thrilled to find out Rosie was pregnant. In a giddy whirlwind the unopened boxes were quickly emptied, their contents finding a home in the kitchen or the closets or onto random shelves. In their place went a crib, a changing table, a children's dresser, and everything else first-time parents need or think they need. Rosie painted two colorful pictures for the baby's room, one of an elephant, the other of a panda, and made sure she hung them when Ron wasn't at home.

When David was born, Rosie and Ron were certain he was the sweetest, most beautiful baby in the world. When he could hold a crayon without shoving it into his mouth, David would sit on the floor in Rosie's studio. While she painted, he scribbled on blank pieces of paper, one moment seriously concentrating and the next joyfully giggling, a smile shining on his face.

On weekends when Ron wasn't working, all three of them would sometimes take a family outing to the grocery store, where David loved toddling alongside Ron. In the paper aisle, Ron would hand him a package of napkins, and David would hold it tightly in his chubby hands as his father lifted him up so he could drop it into the shopping cart. Setting him back down, they both raised their arms and danced in circles while random customers applauded. Though Rosie did refuse to let Ron teach David to steal grapes, plums, or any other produce, it didn't cramp their style in the least. When they returned home, Ron would sit on the floor with David, both laughing as they scribbled outside the lines in the coloring books.

Before they knew it, David was old enough to take apple picking in the fall, sledding in the winter, and kite flying in the spring, while summers were for splashing in Half Moon Lake and building sand castles on the beach. There were also tantrums and tears, lots of hugs, a few stitches, strep throats, and the standard vomiting in the middle of the night. Just because dreams come true doesn't mean they're not going to get messy. Sometimes they even disappear. You wake from one that felt so vivid, only to forget what it was by the time you've poured your first cup of coffee. Dreams can be tricky things.

* * *

It wasn't long before David's favorite place was no longer the grocery store but the neighborhood park. His hair had turned from the light fuzz of babyhood to his mom's golden brown, and his eyes were his father's rich deep brown that sparkled as he laughed with delight when Rosie pushed him on the swings or caught him at the bottom of the slide.

On the rare mornings that Ron was able to join them, he easily undercut the mildest of Rosie's comments like a surgeon with nothing better to do.

Rosie would say, "Isn't this a great park."

Ron would shake his head and chuckle, "Not really," and follow up with "the grass needs mowing" or "the swing set creaks" or "the slide is getting rusty."

She'd say, "What a lovely day." He'd respond with "Why would you say that?" and follow up with "it's pretty cloudy" or "it's too windy" or "it's too hot."

She didn't want to hear that her opinion was wrong any more than necessary, but when soft fluffy clouds slowly floated by, optimist that she was, Rosie always tried again. "Oh, look at those clouds. There's one that looks like a dinosaur and the one over there looks like an angel."

"Rosie," he'd laugh, "you don't know what you're talking about."

* * *

Rosie hadn't done a lot of standing up for herself other than with Greg, which was a biggie. You'd think it would have been a turning point for her, but it wasn't. Nothing had turned. She thought she could handle Ron's dismissive comments and imagined it was like living with someone with a facial tic. It might be irritating but manageable. She was wrong and had no idea of the damage his words were inflicting. Disagreeing with him was exhausting, and she was learning not to offer an opinion unless she knew what it was supposed to be. The trust she had in herself was slowly crumbling. If she'd say the sky is blue, he'd say no it's green, and she'd doubt herself, wondering if maybe it was green though she really thought it was blue.

Rosie continued to hit the snooze alarm whenever it went off in her head. "Wake up, wake up," it buzzed before she silenced it, and in doing so, silenced herself. She never considered that she was becoming Ron's accomplice, doing his job for him, though never quite sure what that job was. Still, she loved him. Why?

* * *

David had his bar mitzvah the winter he turned thirteen, and though Rosie and Ron weren't religious, watching as he chanted prayers and read from the Torah was like seeing centuries of tradition being handed down to a new generation. Ron was puffed up with pride. "That's my son," his posture said. Rosie didn't puff but blinked away tears. The synagogue was filled with family and friends and the regularly attending congregants. Rosie imagined her grandmother sitting among them, safe and free from danger.

* * *

That summer David's sport of choice was baseball. He'd never been interested in basketball, which disappointed Ron. What disappointed him more was that David's team only won a game if it was by accident. Parents sat in the bleachers, visiting with each other and cheering for their children. When the games were over, they headed for the field as the young players, happy and tired, walked toward them, joking and laughing. Particularly frustrated after one game, Ron confronted his son when they returned home. "Why are you playing the game if you don't care if you win?"

"Well, Dad, it's obvious. We play because it's fun and we like to play."

Ron was confused. It was like his son was speaking a foreign language, while Rosie, hearing this from the other room, smiled.

When David was a high school senior, Ron couldn't understand why he wanted to be a teacher and not go into the family business. "After all, I've been building this business for you."

Without rancor, David said, "I love you, Dad, but I have to disagree. You've been building the business for you, and I want to build something, too. I want to build young people's minds so they can think critically, and math is my way to do that."

Ron stared at his son, shook his head, and walked away, as Rosie was coming around the corner from putting in a load of laundry. She'd heard enough of the conversation, and seeing David standing alone, she hugged him, which is quite a feat for any mom with a thirteen-year-old son.

"I'm so proud of you."

"Thanks, I'm hungry."

CHAPTER 10

While David was busy with school, friends, and his part-time job at the Dairy Queen, of course, Rosie continued to paint. Her home studio was a sanctuary, a safe place where she learned to trust her creative decisions, and her mistakes, though sometimes frustrating, were not an issue. They were simply part of the process. It was an oasis where her confidence and trust in herself could safely reemerge, and the number of her completed canvases grew.

In October, Goldie's Art Gallery was looking for works from local artists for their January show. After a focused campaign of encouragement and much nagging from Lou, Patty, and even David, Rosie finally agreed to submit two paintings. One was a horse portrait where she used unexpectedly bold colors to accent the shadows of its face. The other was of a young woman standing in a doorway unsure of whether to walk through it. Much to Rosie's surprise, they were both accepted.

Lou and Patty picked up Rosie for the show's opening night. Ron said he had a late meeting but would get there when he could. Rosie was more nervous than she expected. Once at the gallery, Patty firmly took her hand and pulled her forward until she was standing in front of her paintings. Like all the paintings in the gallery, they each had a small white card with a price next to them, a price that Patty decided on, because Rosie couldn't. Realizing that people would actually see her work, she felt exposed, as if she would be on display, not just her paintings, and her stomach filled with knots.

"I'm not sure if I'm going to cry or throw up."

Knowing she needed a quick distraction, Lou and Patty led her to the back of the gallery where there was a table of appetizers and sweets. Nothing appealed to her until she spotted the mini-chocolate muffins, and any thoughts of tears or nausea immediately disappeared. She planned to eat one as daintily as possible but ended up shoving the entire muffin into her mouth.

"Better?" Lou asked.

"Mmm," she mumbled.

"Okay, let's say hi to your adoring fans."

Before walking away from the table, Rosie grabbed a second muffin and inhaled it, then turned and there was David with his sparkling smile and a hug that always melted her heart.

"I'm so proud of you, Mom. You don't color outside the lines. You create beautiful, powerful new ones."

"Aww, thank you," she said.

"Just so you know, there are a few chocolate crumbs on your cheek."

Embarrassed, she quickly brushed them off as David stepped aside to reveal her proud parents. There was a hug from her mom and a pat on her shoulder from her dad, trying his best not to get emotional.

Next were her brother, Mark, his wife, Cindy, and their two sons. Since hanging out with his cousins was one of David's favorite things to do, and with his new driver's license, he'd be following them home to stay overnight at their house.

"I know I thanked you when we arranged this, but I want to thank you again," Rosie said.

"No need," Cindy smiled. "The boys always have a great time together, and we'll barely notice if there's one more in the house. Plus, he can stay as long as he wants tomorrow so you'll be able to catch your breath from this wonderful and really exciting evening."

Mark added, "We're so thrilled for you, Rosie," as he gently bopped her on the head, and she playfully punched him on the arm.

The gallery was filling up. Rosie was touched to see neighbors and former teacher friends who came to support her. Every once in a while she'd scan the room for

Ron, but he never showed. As things began to quiet down, the crowd thinned, and the artists were able to visit with each other. It's always nice to know you're not alone.

Rosie had lost track of Lou and Patty, but at the end of the evening they reappeared. "We had a great time," Lou said. "Lots of talent hanging on the walls. We talked to some artists, ate, and talked to more artists."

Patty said, "Since Ron never showed up, we're driving you home, but first you'll want to take one more look at your two paintings."

This time, a gentle push was all it took to get Rosie in front of them.

"Do you notice something that wasn't here before?"

"Oh wow, oh wow, oh wow," Rosie stammered.

"Yes!" Lou laughed. "A little red sticker on the wall next to *both* of your paintings, and you know what that means!"

"They've both been sold?"

"They've both been sold!" Lou cheered.

"I can't believe it."

"Well, you'd better believe it! Now you're officially a professional artist."

Patty interjected, "And you'll be selling more. The prints we made of these pieces will now be available for sale in my showroom, thank you very much."

"Oh wow, oh wow, oh wow," Rosie stammered once more. "I don't know what else to say."

"Wow is just fine."

"But wait. I do want to say something else. Thank you both. For everything."

"It was our pleasure."

Then the three of them bundled up, and arm in arm, walked out of the gallery and into the dark, bitter January night.

* * *

Still on a high when she got home, Rosie found Ron sitting on the sofa watching TV.

"How'd it go?" he asked, not taking his eyes off the screen.

There was no way Rosie was going to answer that question and instead said, "You never showed up. Why?"

He reluctantly turned to look at her. "The meeting ran late. Long day. Going up to bed now." He clicked off the TV and disappeared up the steps, and Rosie was left standing alone in the family room.

* * *

The next morning, as Ron was about to leave for work, Rosie walked into the kitchen with her resentment smoldering. She was certain he had purposely avoided the gallery opening and didn't for a moment believe that the meeting ran late, and wondered if there even was a meeting. But, he'd had other late-night meetings, hadn't he? And some evenings he'd play basketball with friends, didn't he? She stopped before considering any other reasons he'd be late coming home.

While trying to decide whether to ignore him, confront him, or, in her deliciously vivid imaginings, punch him, he walked over and surprised her with a kiss. "I was tired last night and a real jerk. I'm so sorry. Love you. Have a great day."

He walked out the door, and she dropped onto a kitchen chair, shaking her head.

That evening, he surprised her with a gift, a beautiful gold necklace that was not her style—and that she never wore.

It's so interesting, Rosie thought, how quickly things return to normal. How does that happen? What is it that pulls a couple back together? Could it be love? It's certainly not the sparkly, shiny kind but the kind that's in dirty sweatpants and a ratty tee shirt, yet somehow still love.

CHAPTER 11

Ron was checking the mail when he found a "save the date" notice for his thirtieth high school reunion in August and rushed to tell Rosie. "Thirty years. Can you believe it? Where did the time go?"

"Thirty years already, huh?"

"I know." He rolled his eyes and chuckled. "Come with me."

"Come with you where?"

"To the reunion."

"Why would I do that, and why would you want me to?"

"Because I love you, and it'll be fun."

"High school reunions are not known for being fun for spouses."

"Oh, come. There are a few couples you already know, and there'll be some great food," and wiggling his eyebrows up and down he added, "including all sorts of chocolate desserts."

"That makes this a tougher decision."

He repeated in a low seductive voice, "choco-lates…ahhh…cho-cooo-laaates."

"All right, all right, okay then!"

"Great. Love ya."

"Me too."

* * *

The reunion was held at the Hillcrest Country Club in Altoona. Rosie felt confident wearing her classic little black dress, with a great pair of turquoise earrings and a matching bracelet. She carried a small clutch that held only lipstick and tissues, not thinking she would need anything more.

Having been out of high school for thirty years, she assumed the attendees were grateful for the dim lighting. High round tables with white tablecloths and small votive candles were scattered around the room. Drinks were available at two bars, each strategically placed in opposite corners. Rosie was certain they'd be much appreciated by everyone, especially by those who had not fit in during high school and were brave enough to attend, and also by the many random spouses who were doing their best not to sneak away or run out of the room screaming.

Rosie was focused on the strategically located buffet tables and was heading straight for the nearest one when Ron took her arm and led her to a couple that she only knew because once, a few years ago, they'd gone to a movie together. The conversation was light with catching up on the basics of family and work. Ron bragged about Rosie's paintings, which surprised her since he took no interest in her art. Another couple soon joined them, and a few minutes later, a lovely brunette walked up to the group wearing a deep blue, rather clingy, low-cut dress that Rosie had to admit looked fabulous on her.

"Hi everyone," she beamed. Everyone immediately responded to her. "Naomi! What a great surprise!" "How've you been?" "Where've you been?" "You look amazing!"

Her smile blossomed from all the attention. "The short version is I just moved back from LA after ending a long-term relationship and found a new job that I love."

"What do you do?" Rosie asked.

"Consulting. It's a great word, isn't it? It can mean anything," she answered, and the group laughed a little too hard.

Rosie was not interested in any more catching-up stories and briefly turned to check out the buffet. Turning back, she saw that Ron and Naomi had disappeared but was not concerned. Saying her good-byes to the two remaining couples, she went to the buffet, filled her plate, and found a high-top table with an empty spot.

"Do you mind if I join you?"

"Not at all," said the kind woman on her left, who looked at her with a sweet but not sappy smile, which is not easy to pull off. She had kind eyes with a little too much blue eye shadow and a black sequined top. "I'm embarrassed to ask, but did you graduate with us and I don't remember? If so, I'm really sorry."

"Oh, please don't worry. I'm a spouse, and my husband has disappeared on me."

"Who's your husband?"

"Ron…." and before she could say his last name, Rosie was interrupted.

"The basketball star?"

"Yep."

"Ah, Ron. We all had serious crushes on him, but that's what you do in high school, right?" The women at the table giggled, and the husbands rolled their eyes.

"Well, welcome. It's nice to meet you." As if on cue, the others joined in with "hi," "hello," or "glad you joined us."

"Will our reminiscing bore you?" asked the sequined-top lady.

"Not at all. I'd love to hear your stories."

"Great! We were just talking about the social studies teacher who was hired only because he was a football coach."

The woman across from her with the largest earrings Rosie'd ever seen continued, "And Judy, I can't remember her last name, anyway, she decided to try an experiment. The class had been assigned a five-page essay, and when she turned hers in, she'd filled pages three and four with nursery rhymes. Because the teacher knew how smart she was, he gave her an A, proving he obviously never read it and probably never read any of the papers that were handed in."

The ex-jock-looking man who had softened around the edges added, "Unfortunately, I can't imagine he read much of anything. I don't think she ever reported him, but if she had, I don't think he'd have gotten much of a reprimand, because, well, he was the football coach."

The man with hair going in every direction and a stain on his tie asked, "How about the teacher who picked his nose and stashed whatever he dug out behind his ear?"

Everyone moaned, and someone said, "Oh gross. I remember him."

Rosie was so entertained by their stories that when a server took her empty plate away, she realized she'd been listening to them for almost an hour. Thanking the group for letting her join them, she excused herself to look for Ron, who was nowhere to be found.

At the nearest bar, she asked for a glass of wine and then remembered she hadn't brought any cash with her. The bartender smiled, said not to worry, and handed her a glass of sparkling water with ice and a lime wedge. Sipping and searching, she took another slow tour around the room looking for her husband. When there was no sighting, Rosie walked out of the ballroom and into the foyer, where she found a comfortable chair next to a table with magazines piled on it, looking like it belonged in a doctor's office waiting room. Flipping through the top one, she found an article on how to find the perfect spouse. Too late, she snorted, then checked the time. It was now almost an hour and a half since she'd seen Ron. What a guy.

All that remained in her drink was a lonely-looking lime wedge and a few not-yet-melted ice cubes, all resting in the bottom of the glass. She didn't want to relate to the lime wedge but couldn't help herself. This was not a good sign. Returning to the ballroom, she handed her glass to a waitress clearing place settings from a nearby table. With her anger building, Rosie scoured the room like a frustrated detective searching for a fugitive and finally spotted her husband in a corner, whispering something into Naomi's ear while she leaned into him, smiling. After they embraced and she walked away, Ron straightened his jacket and moved onto the crowded floor, where he found Rosie staring at him.

"Where were you?" he innocently asked.

Oh boy, he was good, but not that good. "What do you mean where was *I*? Where were *you*?"

"Just talking with Naomi. We wanted to go somewhere private to catch up."

"For over an hour and a half?"

"I didn't realize how much time had gone by. That's the truth."

Ah, a clue. If someone has to say "that's the truth," it's probably not.

"I came with you because you asked me to, and then you *ditched* me. That's incredibly rude and beyond disrespectful."

"I can't believe you're so upset."

"I can't believe you can't understand why," and throwing back to Ron the words he so often used on her, "What's wrong with you?"

"We just wanted to talk. It's not a big deal."

"Don't you pull that on me. It is a big deal. And if you're going to say I'm too sensitive, don't you dare."

He shook his head. "Rosie, if you're that upset, we can go home."

"Yes. Home. I've had enough."

In the silence of the car, it hit Rosie that if she'd had any cash or credit cards with her, she could have taken a cab home or rented a hotel room. She was not going to make that mistake again.

Once home, Ron went up to bed. Rosie stayed downstairs with the wretched 60-inch TV that was too big and too expensive but that Ron insisted they get. When Rosie was sure he was asleep, she got into bed as well, curling up on her side, as far away from him as possible without falling off the edge and holding tightly to tissues that would absorb tears that never came. She'd stood up for herself, which seemed out of character. But was it? Over the years had she molded herself, squeezed herself, into a character that wasn't really her? If so, the seams were beginning to split, and that was not something to cry about.

In the kitchen the next morning, Ron placed a plate of pancakes hot off the griddle in front of her and kissed her on the top of her head. He even cleaned the kitchen afterward, making it clear he knew that he'd really messed up.

CHAPTER 12

Freezing February air followed Ron into the house when he returned from work.

"We have to talk," he hollered as he took off his winter coat.

"What did you say? I'm upstairs working."

He walked to the bottom of the steps and hollered again. "Come down here. We have to talk."

"I'll be there in a couple minutes. I need to clean off my brushes first."

"Well, hurry up."

When she finally joined him at the kitchen table, a frustrated Rosie asked, "Okay, what's going on?"

"I need a home office."

"You already have an office. At work. Why in the world would you need one here?"

"Rosie, I've been thinking about this for a long time. It will be more efficient for me to work on some things here." Without asking or pausing, he added, "and the room that will work best for me is the one you're using."

"What? My studio? No! If you really need one, you can use the extra room off the dining room."

"It's too small."

"How much space do you need?"

"You know I love you and wouldn't ask if it wasn't important. Just move your stuff."

"What did you say?"

"Just move your stuff."

"Are you ordering me around?"

"Sorry, sorry. I'm just feeling so much pressure now that the business is expanding again. Really, I'm so, so sorry about the whole situation."

Rosie did know he was under a lot of pressure, but she was running out of excuses for him. Still, she said "okay" as the voice inside her howled, "NO. NO. NO!"

"Thanks, Rosie." He got up and hugged her. "I know how hard this is for you." Walking out of the kitchen, he turned and said, "By the way, I won't be bringing things over until next Wednesday."

Rosie put her head on the table, cradled by her arms, wondering how she could get that nice girl inside of her to shut up. But it wasn't just the nice girl anymore. She was now joined by the lost girl.

Raising her head, she straightened up and declared, "I'm creative. I can figure this out."

The next morning she got on the phone and called local galleries to see if they knew of any artist studios in the area. That afternoon she drove from one potential location to the next. At the old converted Uniroyal warehouse, she found exactly what she was looking for: individual artist studios, all with huge windows providing amazing light. Even better, there was a small studio available that she could move into as soon as she wanted. That evening she gave Ron the good news.

"Oh," he said, "I thought you'd just store your stuff."

"Why in the world would you think that?"

He shrugged. "Well, isn't it just more of a hobby?"

"Wait a minute. First of all, you should know by now it's not a hobby. Second, why haven't I been a part of this decision-making process to begin with?"

"Rosie, you know that instead of being practical about this, you'd get too emotional."

"I can be emotional and still be practical at the same time. And speaking of practical, what are you giving up?"

Ron shook his head as if he had been trying to explain something complicated to a second grader. "Well, you know any extra money is going back into the business right now, so you'll have to pay the monthly rental fee yourself."

Rosie was furious and felt more of those seams splitting. Walking up the steps to what would soon no longer be her studio, she sat on the floor and closed her eyes. She imagined a vibrant red balloon floating into the sky until Ron began poking it with a small pin. The balloon didn't pop but slowly started to deflate, floating lower and lower. Somehow it repaired itself and began to rise, but each time it started to float up, there was another pinprick, and then another and another. The balloon couldn't repair itself quickly enough and began to get smaller and smaller and drift lower and lower until it was almost on the ground.

Rosie's eyes flashed open. "I will not let this happen to me. Oh, my God!" She grabbed an eleven-by-fourteen-inch canvas and immediately painted a cadmium red balloon, floating untethered in a vast light blue-violet sky.

* * *

After Ron left for work the next morning, Rosie called Lou. "Do you have a minute?"

"Sure."

"Great. HELP!!!!"

"What happened?"

Rosie explained. Lou told her to take a few deep breaths, and she did.

"This isn't helping."

"Well, it was worth a try. Listen, hon, you're smart. There's a solution. Think for a minute. You'll find it."

"Can you give me more than a minute?"

"Sure. Take as long as you need."

"Wow, something just popped into my head. What do you think of this? Mark is a vet for a lot of stables in the area. I could ask if he'd be comfortable connecting me with the ones that have boarders who might be interested in portraits painted of their horses. Even if I did only one a month, my fee would easily cover my rent. Is this crazy?"

"No, it's brilliant, and so are you! You didn't even need a minute, and I say go for it." Then Lou carefully asked, "And may I suggest one more thing."

"Sure, but I have one more thing to say first."

"Okay."

"After I set up appointments at the stables, I'm setting up an appointment with a therapist."

"Oh, I was going to find a way to suggest that if you didn't."

"Ah, great minds. I hope Ron will go with me, but if not, I'm going for myself. Something's not right. Lots of things aren't. Haven't been for a long time, and I'm tired of pretending that they are."

"You can do this, hon. Call me anytime. I'm always here for you."

"Thanks, Lou. Love you."

"Love you too, Rosie."

After a deep breath and long drink of water, she went into the garage to get some empty boxes for packing up her studio. Next to the boxes she found two of her canvases carelessly tossed against the wall and another ripped, lying on the garage floor. Furious once again, or probably still, she immediately called Ron at work. He told her he was just trying to help clean things out, an explanation that didn't come close to working. She abruptly hung up, called her brother, and then tracked down a therapist.

Not surprisingly, the couple's therapy didn't work, but the horse portrait idea worked better than she expected. Along with sharing her information with his clients, Mark reached out to Dan, a successful and recently retired artist who'd supported himself painting horse portraits for over thirty years. Mark gave Rosie Dan's phone number and told her he'd be expecting her call.

* * *

Wednesday Rosie moved into her new studio where she hung her balloon painting on the wall, convinced she'd somehow find a way to pay the rent. Thursday she called Dan, who surprised her by asking if they could meet at her studio the next day. She gratefully agreed and spent the rest of the day eager, nervous, hopeful, anxious, and worrying that he wouldn't think her work was very good. By the time he arrived on Friday, she was exhausted.

Dan was a tall, tanned, sweet, and thoughtful man with a warm smile. After studying her work, he asked if he could forward any future requests he received to her and also share her contact information with previous clients and others who may contact him in the future.

Yawzah!

He also suggested that she check out the American Horse Show Association to find out what upcoming horse shows would be in the area. He explained that he'd built up quite a clientele from horse show competitors, and if she took one or two sample portraits, or even pictures of them, to the shows where owners could see the quality of her work, he had no doubt she'd have a successful business. He also gave her tips on framing and pricing and told her if she had any questions, to call anytime. She floated home and immediately called Mark.

"Dan is wonderful."

"I know."

"He helped me so much."

"That's great."

"I can't thank you enough."

"You're welcome. Anything for my little sister."

Thanks to Mark and Dan, she'd gotten her first three portrait orders almost immediately. For each commission, she'd go to the barn to meet the horses and their owners. Standing a safe distance away from her subjects, she'd take pictures of their faces with her camera and do her best to get a sense of their personalities. After developing her film, Rosie would go to her studio, becoming so focused on her work, she wouldn't notice how much time had gone by until her hand or her back or her eyes told her she needed a break. When that happened, she'd visit other artists in the building. Watching each person creating art in their own unique way was its own kind of therapy and made her braver.

CHAPTER 13

"What? We owe what?"

Looking at Rosie, the accountant repeated, "$15,000. In taxes."

No wonder Ron hadn't wanted her at this meeting and looked panicked when she walked into the office and sat in the chair next to him. Staring across the wide desk in front of them, Rosie did her best to follow what their accountant was saying about payment plans and penalties. When the meeting was over, she followed Ron into the building's small parking lot.

"I have to get back to work," he said, looking at his watch, not at her.

"We need to talk about this as soon as you get home."

"Okay."

"No excuses."

"Okay, okay," he answered, getting into his car and peeling rubber as he drove off.

Rosie was fuming and surprised that the sparks flying out of her weren't lighting the small shrubs edging the parking lot on fire, but it was March, and their small branches were bare.

On her way home, she stopped at the bank, asking for both checking and savings account statements for the past six months. Why hadn't she been doing this regularly? She would be angry with herself later, but right now she had to stay focused.

When they were first married, Rosie paid all the bills. After David was born, she appreciated Ron's offer to take over that job. She'd trusted him and didn't think to question, follow up, or verify what was going on with their money. She mumbled, "I know, I know. A rookie mistake." His financial deception had taken her breath away, and she mumbled again. "I may not have disappeared yet, but our money certainly has."

Ron got home at 7:30 p.m. "I had a meeting that ran late."

Ah, his go-to excuse, Rosie thought. The meeting was probably with himself, to decide how he could once again tell her that she was making too big a deal about something.

He sat down across from her at the kitchen table. She'd found their checkbook in a desk drawer in his recently "acquired" home office. She set it down between them and opened it to the registry showing what checks had been written and the balance remaining.

"I'm assuming you don't believe in psychic banking or simply visualizing your balance."

Ron stared at her.

"There is no balance in the right column. Not on any page. Not anywhere."

"Of course not," he said quite matter-of-factly, insinuating his superiority in financial matters.

"How can you not balance the checkbook, even just once in a while?"

"What's the big deal? That's what Checking Plus is for."

She started to see red, which was appropriate, considering that's where their checking account would soon be. "Well, Ron, that means that when you said we couldn't afford the rent on my studio, you had no idea if we could afford it or not. You simply didn't want me to have it."

He looked at her like a deer caught in headlights.

"Meanwhile, just six months ago you bought a giant one-hundred-inch TV."

"It's eighty-three inches."

She glared at him. "Now onto our savings account, which has a total of $263 in it. You told me that account was to set aside money for taxes, and I gotta tell ya, $263 is not going to do it. What's happened to the money that the business is making?"

"I'm reinvesting it into the company."

"I don't believe you."

"You just don't understand. I knew what was going on with the account. I just didn't know how much was in it or how much I'd taken out."

"Then you didn't know what was going on," she growled. "Why can't you just apologize?"

He couldn't, and he didn't.

"There is something seriously wrong with you. You need to get therapy."

"I will if it will make you feel better."

Geez.

Ron went up to bed and Rosie stayed downstairs. This is backward, she thought. She should have been the one up in the bedroom. Even better, she should have left the house, but she didn't have the strength to go. Instead, she curled up on the family room sofa and covered herself with an afghan. She didn't want to think anymore and turned on the five-hundred-inch TV she hated.

* * *

Rosie desperately needed to get away to sort things out, to sort herself out, and made reservations for a three-night stay at the Lowell Inn, about an hour and fifteen minutes away in Stillwater, Minnesota. Every summer when she and Mark were young, their parents would take them to visit the small river town for a weekend vacation. It was there that they had, what they still consider to be, the best ice cream cones ever. For Rosie, this memory was a compelling enough reason to return, even though it was March and any ice cream shop wouldn't open until at least mid-April.

As she tossed her overnight bag into the car's back seat, the gray sky was releasing a fine drizzle, matching Rosie's mood. The trees were bare. The crisp, sparkling winter snow had melted into small grime-covered patches, revealing earth that was hard and dark. It looked like life hadn't survived the winter—that it tried but couldn't hold on. Everything seemed hopeless and cold. Rosie could relate. No rebirth could be seen happening anytime soon and had to be taken on faith, a faith that Rosie could not access.

Noticing that the car's gas gauge was close to empty, she stopped to fill up. Such a simple thing. When Rosie pulled away from the gas pump, her vision blurred, whether from tears or tension she couldn't tell. She pulled into a spot next to the station's convenience store, leaned back in her seat, closed her eyes, and there it was. The memory.

The summer after David's junior year of college, he was sharing an apartment near campus with two friends and had gotten a new job as a waiter at Woo's Pagoda Restaurant, hoping for some great tips and possibly free egg rolls.

When Rosie told him that she and Ron were considering taking a ten-day road trip, David thought it was a wonderful idea. Rosie considered asking him to check in with her parents while they were gone but knew that wouldn't be necessary, since they'd definitely be checking in with him.

* * *

Ron and Rosie drove west from Wisconsin through Minnesota and South Dakota, where they imagined the conversation pioneer couples had when they reached the Black Hills. "This doesn't look good."

"I told you not to turn left at the river!"

Apparently, even then men didn't like having someone give them directions.

In Wyoming, they turned south onto a two-lane highway with less traffic and more scenery. When something inspired or intrigued them, they'd pull off to investigate, getting out of the car to explore or simply sitting on the hood, holding hands, and quietly taking in the view. Stopping in small towns, they'd find a local diner and sit at the counter, spinning on their red vinyl seats until their burgers appeared, then walk down Main Street, browse in thrift shops, and visit with the owners.

Traveling further south, the summer heat intensified. Even with the air conditioning on, it shimmied its way into the car. The air dried out and so did the land. The scenery turned rocky, desolate, harsh, and strikingly bold. It wouldn't have surprised Rosie to see a lone weathered cowboy riding in the distance. But there was no one. She saw only sagebrush and cactus and a gas station standing like a sentinel, a warning, "Last chance before going into the wilderness."

"Let's stop for gas," said Rosie.

"No. We're fine."

"Our gas gauge is registering almost empty. I'd feel better if we stopped."

"Not necessary."

"Stop. Please."

"Rosie, we're fine, don't worry."

"Ron, we don't know when there'll be another gas station. We don't even know when we'll see another car on this road."

"Don't be silly," was his final response. He sped right by it, and the gas station quickly faded away.

She couldn't have felt more worthless or powerless if he'd slapped her across the face. Staring out the side window at the hard land and the hard blue sky above it, Rosie shrunk into herself. Whenever they'd go over a hill or around a curve she'd turn, and looking forward, strain to see any signs of life, but there was nothing. Fifteen minutes later they hadn't seen another car, and the gas gauge was now past empty. When the red warning light started blinking, Rosie prayed that the next miles were all downhill. Otherwise, she expected vultures to be circling in the not-too-distant future.

It was ten more long minutes before she saw two buildings, like a mirage, far in the distance.

"Rosie, I told you we'd be fine," Ron said as they coasted into an intersection, empty except for the gas station and a liquor store.

"I should hit you and then hit the liquor store," she replied, gritting her teeth and staring straight ahead.

Ron laughed and got out of the car to pump gas. Rosie got out and took a short walk down the road, feeling battered and worthless.

When Rosie returned to the station, Ron was inside paying for the gas and getting some snacks. The minute she climbed back into the car, a large hawk swooped low, coming so close to the windshield that she could see its yellow eyes. For an instant, it stared right at her. She stared right back, then watched as it soared into a brilliant blue sky. Rosie'd felt shock but not fear. She'd certainly felt seen. She knew something powerful had just happened and that there was an important message in this experience. Was it a message meant to lift her up, to sustain her until she could learn to fly herself? If so, that would be a long time coming. She never forgot this gift, for that's what she felt it was, and never shared it with Ron.

Now here she was, almost ten years later, on a chilly March Day in Wisconsin, sitting in another car, having pumped her own gas. Opening her eyes, Rosie looked up at the sky, and far in the distance, just below the heavy gray clouds, there it was, a hawk gliding on a current of air.

CHAPTER 14

It was late in the afternoon, and Rosie was making good time on her drive, being careful not to speed through the small town of Menomonie where the police were always cheerfully waiting to write you a ticket. Driving through the larger town of Hudson, she crossed the dark, choppy waters of the St. Croix River and into Minnesota. Turning right, she followed the river north and fifteen minutes later was on Stillwater's Main Street, slowly passing antique shops and craft stores, restaurants and art galleries. In a short time, she turned left, and in one block arrived at the Lowell Inn. It was an older, yet still elegant, three-story building, white with black shutters. It reminded Rosie of a gracious lady who had been keeping herself well-maintained though her youth had passed. She loved that it had a history. There were stories resting inside those walls that gave it an intriguing sort of character. Rosie held over fifty years of stories inside herself as well and wondered if that made her intriguing too, in a Greta Garbo sort of way, or if it simply meant she was often dealing with hot flashes and having trouble finding her car keys.

Parking in the hotel lot, she deliberately zipped her keys into the side pocket of her purse, tossed her jacket over her shoulders, picked up her overnight bag, and walked into the building. On her right, floor-to-ceiling doors opened to a large dining room. On her left, there was a long open lobby where overstuffed chairs were strategically placed to create conversation areas, looking like soft comfortable chess pieces on a carpeted game board. Straight ahead was a small registration desk where a blonde college-age receptionist greeted her. She seemed not to fit the mood of the place. Rosie expected someone more matronly, more familiar, who would knowingly pat her hand and give her a comforting smile. Instead, she was welcomed with perky.

"I see your reservation is for three nights. That's great!" the receptionist bubbled. "You have the Blue Room on the second floor. That's wonderful!" she cheered. "Enjoy your stay with us!" She bubbled once more and handed Rosie her room key.

The greeting was like an ice-cold Dairy Queen Strawberry Slush, refreshing but giving you an instant headache between your eyes and reminding Rosie that old buildings don't need to have old spirits.

Her room was named correctly. The carpet was royal blue, the walls were a light dusty blue, the ruffled curtains were cornflower blue. The beige bedspread, edged with a pattern of delicate pink and yellow flowers with pale green leaves, was a relief. Not wanting to be left out of the action, a narrow cornflower blue ribbon matching the curtains wove gently through them.

Rosie panicked for a moment when she realized there was no TV in the room, then grudgingly decided that was fine. Staring at it would be an acceptable creative avoidance. Well, not really creative, but definitely an avoidance, and she'd been avoiding things for too long.

Looking out the window, she couldn't see the river, only the office building across the street, but she knew the river was there, and that was enough for her. It was a luxury, in fact. Too often she had stared at dirty dishes piled in the sink, dirty clothes tossed in a laundry basket, furniture that hadn't been dusted, windows that hadn't been cleaned, and when she was teaching there were lessons that needed to be planned. Though she never rushed her painting, everything else around her was a reminder that she was behind and needed to move, often when she shouldn't move at all. So it was a luxury to simply look out a window on a gray day after the rain had stopped, even if she couldn't see the river.

Rosie left her overnight bag by the bed and shoved her arms into her jacket. Zipping it up and grabbing her purse, she headed out into the sharp air for an early dinner. Walking back to Main Street, she turned left, passed two antique shops, and found a casual restaurant. Near the entrance was a bakery case filled with all things chocolate and glazed, waiting to be chosen, bagged, and sent home with someone. She'd definitely found the right place.

It seemed safe here. Rosie couldn't imagine bumping into anyone she knew, and at barely 5:00 p.m., it wasn't crowded. At one table there were two young college-age girls. At another, a handsome gray-haired man was sitting with his wife. She assumed it was his wife. Maybe she shouldn't assume that anymore. Lately, she'd been thinking about Ron's basketball pick-up games, wondering if that was all he'd been picking up. She couldn't imagine he'd betray her that way and quickly put it out of her mind.

The soup and salad special she ordered was delicious. The potato soup was thick and creamy, and the sandwich was piled so high with tuna fish, lettuce, and tomato that she could have taken half of it back to her room for later but, always up for a challenge, she ate the entire thing. While her tongue pried a piece of lettuce out from between her cheek and her back teeth, she wondered if she should feel guilty spending money on this getaway, but to her it felt like a last gulp of air before going under.

By 6:30 p.m., she was back in her hotel room sitting on the bed with her shoes kicked off and opening the complimentary mini-bottle of wine that had been left on the nightstand along with two cookies, a chocolate chip and an oatmeal, which was great because she'd forgotten to take any bakery treats from the restaurant.

After munching on cookies and sipping wine she called Lou, who picked up after the first ring. "Rosie?"

"Yep."

"How's it going?"

"My world is upside down. I just ate two cookies and liked the oatmeal one better than the chocolate chip. What's happening to me?"

Lou laughed. "I can't imagine!"

"Now that I'm here, I'm not quite sure what to do next."

"You'll figure it out."

"Thanks, I hope so. I know I definitely have to do something about that 'Nice Girl' thing. It's really messed me up."

"It does that to a lot of us. It should probably come with a Surgeon General's warning."

"Ah, yes, I see it now. Handle with care. If not used wisely, you can 'nice' yourself into oblivion. It's not as dramatic as being blown to bits but just as effective. Either way, you are gone."

"You know," Lou said, "I read somewhere that there is a difference between being nice and being kind."

"What is it?"

"I have no idea."

"Something to ponder since I have no TV."

"No TV! What will you do?"

"Ponder. I have lots of pondering to do."

"There ya go. You know I'm always here for you. I only have one request."

"What?"

"While you're there, buy something for yourself. It can be something small, but it has to be just for you. And cookies don't count."

"Oh no!"

"Oh yes!"

"Okay," Rosie sighed.

"Promise?"

"Yes, and thanks. I feel better, and you know I love ya."

"Love ya, too."

After hanging up, Rosie called downstairs to order a room service breakfast and was told they would only have sweet rolls and coffee, which sounded great to her. Next she got into her nightshirt and shook her head. It was embossed with a little bee and the phrase bee-lieve in yourself. Ugh, a motivational nightshirt. Just what I need.

CHAPTER 15

The next morning Rosie sat in her blue room enjoying two freshly baked and still-warm caramel rolls, a small bowl of fresh fruit, and a small pot of coffee. Then bundling up for the day's outing she headed back to Main Street. Finding a local bookstore, she walked right in with a contented sigh. For Rosie, being in a bookstore had always felt like being in a candy store—so many delicious things to read. Unfortunately, Rosie'd become so self-conscious over the years, she had no doubt she'd be judged according to where she browsed by the few strangers in the store who she'd never see again. Of course, she would be found lacking. In what, it didn't matter.

She found a section of self-help books that she could probably use but wasn't interested. She'd read plenty of them but lately had become very tired of personal growth. It was like being at the gym with a trainer insisting you do something about the self-delusional butt that you've become quite fond of. She wasn't interested in biographies either. She was having enough trouble figuring out her own life and didn't want to deal with someone else's. Romance? Ha! Forget it! Mysteries were acceptable, and the classics were always safe.

For some reason, she found herself in the children's section looking at fairy tales. Cinderella leaves a bad home situation and quickly runs to a prince without thinking about the consequences. Snow White and Sleeping Beauty wait for a prince to wake them up, but that was their job. Rosie sympathized. She was learning how painful and frightening waking up can be. Then there's dear Rapunzel. Feeling trapped in a high tower, she believes the only way to escape is to cut off the part of herself that is magic. It made Rosie want to cry. She didn't remember how the story ended, but she knew it would not end well.

* * *

Without any purchases, Rosie stepped back into the chilly March day. Wandering into a few small antique stores and a gift shop where she fulfilled her promise to Lou and bought two five-inch-high angel ornaments, one for each of them. Small though they were, it couldn't hurt to have an angel hanging around, even if it was ornamental.

When she found herself in front of Darla's Cafe, Rosie was ready for lunch. Her burger and fries arrived along with a chocolate malt topped with whipped cream and a cherry. You don't often see that much attention to detail anymore.

She had chosen to sit in one of the booths along the side wall. It felt less conspicuous than a table in the middle of the room. At one of those tables was a mom and dad and three young children. Watching them for a moment, Rosie wondered if the dad ever said "I'm sorry" to his wife. At another table was a couple that seemed to be in their seventies. Imagining what she and Ron would be like together at that age, she got a deep chill, and it wasn't from the malt.

After lunch, she strolled through too many craft shops smelling of too many fragranced candles, and by early afternoon was back in her blue room. She did miss having a TV but had her own drama going on at the moment, thank you very much. She thought of all the made-for-TV movies she'd watched over the years and how she always wanted to yell at the female leads. "How can you not see what's going on? What is wrong with you?!" Sinking down onto the bed, she moaned. "How did *I* not see what was going on? What is wrong with *me*?" Curling up on her side and closing her eyes, she heard a rushing in her ears. At first she thought it might be her shame, but her shame was much chattier. Rosie sensed it was her anger. She wondered if it would creep slowly toward her like a fog or hit her like a freight train, if she would trip over it like a crack in the sidewalk or fall into it like a ditch on the side of the road.

In the past when she'd had small bursts of anger, she'd quickly lock them away, somehow convinced that being angry made her a bad person. She hadn't understood that her anger, like the alarm in her head, was just trying to warn her. "Pay attention. Something's wrong. Pay attention." Her anger was now huge and shoving it away was no longer an option. She felt it coming closer, like an iceberg, and worried it would sink her to the bottom of a cold, dark sea, but then dared to wonder if, instead of an iceberg, it was a sturdy life raft, and it was coming to her rescue. Wouldn't that be wonderful.

As much as she tried, she wasn't able to nap and laid in that not-quite-asleep mode for the afternoon. Feeling too drained to go out for dinner, she ordered room service again. A half-hour after it arrived, so did her complimentary wine and cookies. What a wild night she was having, and putting on her motivational nightshirt reminded her to put in her breakfast order for caramel rolls and coffee.

* * *

The next morning, the kitchen called to say they were having issues and would not be able to bring her breakfast.

"They think they're having issues," she mumbled, bundling up and walking to the Starbucks on Main Street where she ordered black coffee and a blueberry muffin and settled at a small table in an alcove by a window. The bright sunlight gave the illusion that it was warming the bone-chilling March air. It was not.

Watching the little bits of traffic go by, Rosie felt herself doing a Tarzan swing from energizing anger to debilitating grief and back again, but knowing she was more like Jane, just trying to hang on.

Her "shoulda, woulda, couldas," which are always such a treat, were having a field day scurrying around in her head and slamming into her fragile self-worth.

"Knock it off!" Rosie silently hollered at them, but they didn't have any sympathy for her. She imagined them grinning and teasing, "You can't catch us. You can't catch us." Argh! Drained, she stopped hollering, stopped playing the game, and simply watched them from the bleachers. Interestingly, it wasn't long until all she heard was silence.

From her oversized purse, she pulled out a spiral notebook and dug around to find a pen. Rosie was ready to journal, but her pen felt too heavy to hold, and she set it down.

There must have been good times. Why couldn't she remember them? She didn't think they were lost, just buried for a while. Had Ron ever loved her? She believed he had, but so much of what she had believed was turning out not to be true. Maybe he was carrying a deep pain that he'd hidden, not only from her but from himself. She wondered if he was also struggling or simply frustrated that she was no longer compliant and unwilling to let him get away with anything else.

Walking sluggishly back to the inn and not ready to return to her room, Rosie got into her car and drove out of the parking lot. She headed north and then west, passing barren trees and empty fields and exploring small random neighborhoods. Even with the cold sunshine, the scenery was definitely not lifting her spirits. After an hour, she found herself in the charming town of White Bear Lake, located at the edge of the mostly frozen waters of, yes, White Bear Lake. She strolled the streets, worked up an appetite, and since she'd missed lunch, was ready for another early dinner. At the Keys Cafe, she ordered a comforting hot turkey blue plate special, and once back at the Lowell Inn, room service called to assure her that she'd get her two caramel rolls with coffee in the morning. The kitchen had resolved its issues. She should be so lucky.

* * *

The next morning it was time for Rosie to head home. With her overnight bag in the back seat of the car, her to-go cup of coffee in its holder, and what was left of her second caramel roll in a small paper bag on the seat next to her, Rosie drove away. Yesterday's bright sun had disappeared, and gray drizzle had returned. The closer she got to Eau Claire, the slower she drove. Reaching the outskirts of the city, she slowed down even more by exploring random side streets and finding herself in unfamiliar neighborhoods. She noticed a small park that reminded her of the one she'd go to with David when he was little and stopped at the curb to sit quietly for a few moments.

There was a single, very familiar, car in the park's small lot. Pressed against the passenger side window was a woman in a passionate embrace with someone also very familiar. If it had been a movie, the windows would be steaming up and the car would be rocking. Rosie couldn't help herself. She walked over, opened the passenger side door, and watched as Ron and the woman tumbled out. Turning her back on the jumble of limbs, she returned to her car. Driving away, she noticed the street sign. She was on Revelation Road. Beneath it was a smaller sign. No Exit.

Ain't that the truth.

CHAPTER 16

Across from each other once again at the kitchen table, Rosie was in sweats with her hair pulled back into a ponytail, and Ron was in jeans, wearing a sweater she'd never seen before. He didn't reach across and try to hold her hand, which was good because she would have considered breaking it. She'd never do such a thing but appreciated the thought and the anger that inspired it. Ron didn't mention the incident at the park. Either he didn't see Rosie and thought it had been some teenage prank, or he knew it was Rosie and thought if he didn't mention it, it didn't happen, just like a cat who thinks if it doesn't look at you, you're not there.

"This is really hard for me, but my therapist said it was important that I speak honestly to you about all I've done." said Ron. His voice constricted, and he took a sip of water to clear his throat.

Rosie placed her hands in her lap, clasping them tightly together while her shoulders tensed and her stomach knotted. He'd been seeing a therapist after all. This should be interesting.

Ron confessed to mismanaging their finances and then took five minutes to justify what he'd done, explaining that he never meant to deplete their marital trove.

Marital trove? Are you kidding?

He confessed to three affairs, one of which went on for over a year.

Rosie cringed. Her instincts were right about those basketball pick-up games. When she asked, he told her the women's names, which not surprisingly included high school Naomi, then ridiculously took another five minutes explaining that they never meant anything and how much he loved her.

After another sip of water, he wiped his eyes. "I've cleared my conscience and told you everything."

"No you haven't."

"Of course I have."

"No. You haven't."

"Yes. I have."

Determined to stop this back and forth, she insisted, "That's not true. In fact, I was recently given the name of someone else you were sleeping with." It was a lie, but she couldn't help herself.

"That can't be."

Rosie just stared at him until he said, "Tell me who she is, and I'll tell you if you're right."

He was so busted, and Rosie felt she was shattering into a million pieces. It was clear that she'd never learn the total number of women he had been with, and it really shouldn't have mattered, but somehow it did. Who was this man, and what happened to the person she married? The man who charmingly colored outside the lines had, at some point, tossed the coloring book and crayons into the trash and never looked back.

It took all her strength to hold herself together and calmly ask him to leave the house. Calmly? How did she do that? Avoiding eye contact, he left without saying a word. Rosie should have left too, but she couldn't move. When she finally could, she headed for the shower feeling filthy.

With water as hot as she could manage pounding on her, she scrubbed and cried and screamed. She waited for guilt to raise its ugly head, which it certainly would. It would whisper, "Somehow this must all be your fault. How did you not know? How did you keep yourself from knowing?"

Rosie moaned a heartbreaking moan. "What's going to become of me?"

Startled, she felt a sudden smack between her shoulder blades and heard a very irritated voice. "What do you mean? What's going to become of you? Your life is going to finally become *YOUR* life. After all I've done for you, don't you get it? This is a good thing. So, knock it off."

"What the…? Who's there?"

No one, of course. Rosie wondered if she had a royally pissed off angel who'd been watching over her. Are angels even allowed to get pissed off? She had no other way to explain what had just happened. Unsettled and immobilized, she stood planted in the shower until she heard the voice again, gentler this time. "Hang in there, kiddo. You can do this."

Rosie was sitting up in bed when Ron returned and walked into the bedroom. "Rosie, I know you're very angry," he said unusually timidly.

Her voice was low and still surprisingly calm. "Yes, I am." What kind of an answer is that from someone who's just found out they have been betrayed for much of their married life? "This is no way to be angry. Where did my anger go? Come back, come back!" she silently pleaded. Rosie imagined it returning and igniting a fuse that sputtered along until it reached its destination, and the nice lady blinks, and kablooey, crash, bam. The neighbors three doors down hear the explosion, nod, and sigh, "Ah, it's about time."

Rosie told Ron to sleep in David's old room, and the next day she told him to move out, both of which he did.

* * *

As soon as he was gone, she called Lou and tearily invited her and Patty over for comfort and support and "the marriage is over" pizza. They arrived with huge hugs and a grocery bag filled with sodas and boxes of tissues.

Lou with her Coke, Patty with her Diet Coke, and Rosie with her Dr Pepper sat down at the kitchen table where the two large veggie pizzas Rosie had ordered were waiting. There's something about the saucy, cheesy smell of a pizza that can usually activate almost any appetite, but not Rosie's. Not today.

Realizing that Lou and Patty had been unusually quiet, she said, "Have you been waiting for me to dump all over you?"

They nodded.

"Well, I should get this out of my system."

Lou said, "Very wise. And I wouldn't call it dumping. How about sharing, explaining, releasing?"

Patty said, "Nah, it's dumping. Dumping works for us, and we won't even interrupt you."

"You're right, Patty. Go for it, Rosie."

"Okay, don't say I didn't warn you."

First she dumped the financial betrayals on them, much of which they already knew. Next came the sexual betrayals. "You know I was probably scrubbing the toilet while he was out screwing his receptionist and Ms. Whoever Else. And I was probably washing his underwear when he was buying gifts for Ms. Random Chickie. But, believe it or not, those things weren't even the worst. The worst was realizing that I was laying down night after night next to someone who, consciously or not, was attempting to slowly crush my spirit and destroy my dreams."

Covering her face with her hands, Rosie sobbed. Lou pushed the tissue box close to her elbow. She and Patty waited patiently, watching as the used tissues piled up on the floor around Rosie, like a small, soggy snowdrift.

Eventually, Rosie came up for air, wiped her tears, and noisily blew her nose. "How could I have misjudged him so terribly? What's wrong with me?" She blew her nose again and took a long swallow of Dr Pepper.

"Nothing is wrong with you," Patty insisted.

"I think he was playing some sort of game, seeing how much he could get away with," said Rosie. "It seemed he always needed to win, but why? What did he think he was winning? I thought we were partners. Marriage isn't supposed to be a competition."

"This is something you could not have controlled or changed," offered Patty. "This comes from a wounded, damaged place somewhere deep inside of him."

"I wonder if I sensed that, and it's the reason I made excuses for him for so many years. He brought his wounds into our marriage, just as I did mine, and either his were so severe, he didn't care, or didn't even realize, that he was visiting them on me."

"You can't heal from something you won't acknowledge," added Lou.

Rosie nodded, "Makes me sad for him. Still angry. Very, very angry. But sad."

"Better?" Lou asked.

"A little, yes." And when Patty added, "You just have to hang in there like a hair in a biscuit," Rosie giggled.

"Seriously though," Patty said, "I think he's one of those people who mistake kindness for weakness, and one thing you are not is weak."

Rosie couldn't hear the compliment and instead asked, "What am I going to do with all this anger? It's overwhelming me."

"Accept it," said Lou. "If you don't, it will be constantly trying to get your attention. And then thank it. It's gotten you moving."

"And be sure you use it wisely," instructed Patty, "which doesn't include pushing anyone off a bridge."

"How about I start with filing for divorce?"

Patty agreed, "Great choice, and it won't get you arrested."

CHAPTER 17

Exhausted, and with an ear infection, Rosie arrived at her parents' early Tuesday evening for the Passover Seder. Not only was it her favorite holiday, but other than the matzah and gefilte fish, it was also her favorite holiday meal. The Seder tells the story of how Moses led the Israelites out of Egypt, from slavery to freedom. It is a reminder that freedom is precious and comes with the responsibility to protect it, for ourselves and for others. How could anyone not love this holiday?

Rosie decided to pretend she was doing well. In her experience, family gatherings weren't always the safest place, to be honest. Being with her critical, accepting, judgmental, loving family was confusing and challenging enough. It was also quite wonderful. And loud. Tonight, there would be lots of laughter and, as always, a few political arguments sprinkled into the conversation to spice things up.

Walking through the front door, comforting smells embraced her with memories of holidays past. Her dad waved from the sofa while continuing to explain to any-one who would listen why he was right about the newest proposed legislation. She waved back, and suddenly her cheek was trapped by the firm pinch of her Aunt Miriam's fingers. At eighty-two, she still had quite a grip, and her hair, permanently sprayed within an inch of its life, was harder than a stale bagel.

"Oye, I can't imagine what you must be going through. Are you eating enough? I don't think you're eating enough. Can I get you some chopped liver? It's so good you could just plotz."

"No thanks. I'm fine, and how are you?"

"Well, my bursitis is acting up, and I have pain in my left foot from my bunions, and my eyes…"

Coming to the rescue, her husband, Uncle Murray, quietly appeared. He was smaller than Aunt Miriam in both height and girth, and not quite as put together. His trademark bow tie, purple today, was always a little crooked, and his fine hair was constantly floating in different directions. There was a sadness in his blue eyes from the horrors he had seen as a young man in Poland. Yet even with that history, his smile was always warm and welcoming. He interrupted his wife by giving Rosie a gentle hug and winked at her before turning to Aunt Miriam.

"Miriam, dear, can you show me where the chopped liver is?"

"Oh, Murray, you'll love it. It's so good, you could just plotz."

As arm in arm, Miriam and Murray headed for the highly acclaimed appetizer, Rosie went to help out in the kitchen but found that her mom and her mom's sister, Aunt Lyla, had everything under control. The chicken soup was simmering on the stove, the brisket was heating in the oven, and nothing had spilled, dripped, or spattered on either of them. How could that be possible? Rosie couldn't make a peanut butter and jelly sandwich without some peanut butter stuck in her hair and drops of jelly on her clothes.

After the hugging, Aunt Lyla began her usual critique.

"Look at you. So beautiful, but you have to do something with your hair. That green sweater just doesn't work for you. What kind of green is that anyway? You could use more blush and a brighter lipstick, and what's with those earrings?"

Rosie's mom diplomatically interrupted, "We're in good shape here and…"

"Yes, all under control," Aunt Lyla interrupted right back. Saying I love you to Rosie, she shooed her out of the kitchen.

Turning back, Rosie said, "Love you both, too," and her mom smiled with a shrug that meant, "Well, what can ya do, that's my sister."

* * *

It was warmer than usual for late April, and Rosie walked out to the backyard patio where she found Aunt Sophie smoking one of her non-filtered Camel cigarettes. Aunt Sophie had always scared her just a bit. She was not quite five feet, built like a solid square, with thick glasses, and tightly permed white hair. Now in her early seventies, she was still as tough as nails and not someone you'd want to mess with. No one knew exactly how she was related, and no one was brave enough to ask. She was quite good at babysitting small children since they instinctively knew not to misbehave. But while the little ones napped, she often rearranged their parents' living room furniture, dragging anything she didn't like into the backyard and could never understand why it upset anyone or why her babysitting jobs never lasted.

Staring intently at Rosie, she didn't say hello, but after taking a deep drag of her cigarette and exhaling, she came right to the point. "Did anyone ever tell you the story about your grandmother and the rug?"

"What? No."

"You know she was born in Lithuania, right?"

Rosie nodded yes.

"You know how dangerous it was there and about the terrifying random attacks on Jewish settlements."

Rosie nodded again. "The pogroms."

"Yes. When your grandmother was a little girl, and news that an angry mob was approaching, her parents would roll her up in a rug and put the rug on the highest shelf in their small home."

"I didn't know."

"I'm not surprised. Your grandmother rarely talked about it. Can you imagine the fear she must have felt?"

"No."

"Later, as a teenager, she fled with her family to the United States. I was told that the immigration agent on Ellis Island couldn't pronounce their last name, so he gave them a new one. Hope. She became Rachel Hope. She met your grandfather here and started a new life in a new country, not knowing the language and separated from everything familiar. Can you imagine the courage that took?"

"No."

"She carried with her both fear and courage. You are like your grandmother that way, and though she was never able to set down her fear, I believe you will."

Aunt Sophie stared hard at Rosie. "Do you understand what I'm telling you?"

"I think so. Yes."

Aunt Sophie took a final drag on her Camel, tossed it on the ground and stomped it out with her heavy black orthopedic shoes. "Okay then. I'm going inside for some more chopped liver."

Rosie was left standing alone. Her grandmother had passed away when Rosie was fourteen. When she and Mark were little, they'd sleep overnight at her house. She'd treat them to a cup of hot chocolate in heavy chipped mugs and then tuck them into their beds, each curling up under one of her beautiful handmade quilts. When she passed away, their mom made sure they each were given the quilt under which, feeling safe and loved, they'd slept and dreamed young dreams.

Rosie imagined her grandmother as a little girl, rolled into a rug and hidden on that high shelf. How hard must it have been for her to breathe? Hearing shots or cries or screams, how hard must she have prayed? Were her arms pinned tightly against her sides or were her elbows bent so her hands rested against her face?

Rosie looked down at her own hands wondering if her fingers were the same shape her grandmother's had been. Was fear passed on like the shape of fingers or big feet or dimples, or was it handed down like silver candlesticks or a diamond brooch? Was there an energy that carried it from generation to generation? Would this fear Rosie inherited save her life or destroy it, be a blessing or a curse? If it was a curse, was it something she could return, even if she didn't have a receipt, or even if it was slightly used, if she explained, "I'm sorry, but this just doesn't work for me." Maybe it would be better if she kept it around. One day it might be just what she'd need.

Rosie's mother had no rug in which to roll her up. Instead, to keep her safe she rolled her up in conformity, making sure she had the right haircut, the right clothes, and the right friends. Rosie had always thought that her mom was being superficial, and her eyes filled with tears as she realized the only way her mother thought she could protect her daughter was to make sure she fit in and hide in plain sight like Superman or Wonder Woman.

Ron had also done his best to find ways to roll her into a rug and put her on a shelf, but it was never to protect her.

Ah, but Aunt Sophie also used the word courage and that too, was passed on. Is each generation given the opportunity to move from fear to courage, from slavery to freedom. When Rosie was little, she used to think it would be nice to have a Moses lead the way, but now she had something better. She had her grandmother.

CHAPTER 18

The patio door opened, and her brother walked out wearing khaki pants and a blue shirt that matched his eyes. His thick light brown hair was damp, as if he'd recently gotten out of the shower.

"Running a little late. Horses don't do appointments."

"Your timing is perfect. I could really use a hug right now," she said, and he gave her a big one.

"Did anyone ever tell you what a great brother you are?"

"Ha! Yah, you did."

"Well, let me say it again."

"Not necessary, Rosie. What's going on…other than a nasty divorce?"

"Just had a conversation with Aunt Sophie."

"Oh, boy."

"Yep. Did you know the story about Grandma being rolled up in a rug?"

"Sure. Didn't you?"

"Never heard it before."

"That's weird."

"Well, it kinda sucks that I didn't know."

"It does," Mark nodded, looking carefully at his sister. "So, how're you doing?"

"I'm okay."

"Really?"

"Well, not really, but I will be."

He smiled. "And David, how's he doing?"

"He's made some great friends in Madison, and they're all having a seder together tonight. He's slowly working toward his master's in mathematics and thinks he wants to continue teaching high school. When students ask him why math's important, he tells them that without it, we couldn't travel to galaxies far, far away, and he considers it a miracle when there are some smiles and a few heads nod. But that's not what you were asking about, was it?"

Mark shook his head.

"Okay. Well, you already know that telling him I'd filed for divorce was the hardest phone call I'd ever had to make." Then she smiled. "I'm so proud of him. He seems to be handling it with a wisdom beyond his years. He calls to ask what I need, and I tell him I don't need a thing. He tells me to take care of myself and that he loves me. I tell him I love him, too. We hang up, and I cry."

"You raised a wonderful young man, Rosie."

"Thanks." After a deep sigh she asked, "Speaking of wonderful, how about your family?"

Mark told her the boys were great, both still working in San Francisco, no romantic possibilities, and going to their cousin Joanie's for the Seder. His wife, Cindy, decided to go to Green Bay to be with her mom, because it would be her mom's first holiday alone, since her dad passed away.

"You didn't go?"

"Nope. She insisted I stay here, because this is your first holiday alone, too." He smiled and gently bopped Rosie on the head, and she playfully punched him on his arm. They walked back into the house just as their dad hollered, "I'm hungry. Let's get this show on the road," and joined the twelve people flocking to find seats at the table like birds maneuvering to find the best spot at a freshly filled bird feeder.

Mark quickly found a seat and grinned at Rosie from across the table as she found herself between Aunt Sophie on her right and Aunt Miriam on her left. After a very abbreviated version of the required Passover story and prayers, and the partaking of the symbolic food and wine, the meal began in earnest. Rosie's mom and aunt sprung into action, insisting Rosie stay seated when she started rising to help.

First came the chicken soup with matzah balls. It was tradition to use her grandmother's matzah ball recipe, even though they always turned out so hard in the middle that they didn't float in the soup but lay on the bottom of the bowl like a very small shipwreck. When trying to cut through one with your soup spoon, it wasn't unusual for it to fly out of the bowl and bounce across the table.

Next came the main course, starting with the always delicious brisket.

"How long did you have to cook this to get it so tender?" Aunt Sophie asked.

"Almost twelve hours," said Aunt Lyla.

"Hmm," she said, lowering her voice and staring at Rosie through her thick glasses. "So, with enough time, tough things do turn tender and, eventually, even delicious."

Rosie had to give her credit. She'd never heard that cooking a brisket could be used for inspiration and encouragement. Well done, Aunt Sophie.

Toward the end of the meal, Rosie's mom gave her "the look."

"Have some more brisket."

"No thanks."

"How about some more potatoes? I know how much you love potatoes."

"No thanks."

"Just a few. Take just a few."

"I don't want any more."

"Another popover?"

Rosie shook her head.

"There's still some chopped liver left."

* * *

When Rosie returned home that evening, she found her grandmother's quilt. Of all places, it was on the top shelf in the bedroom closet. She carefully took it down and covered herself with it as she lay on her bed and fell asleep reflecting on fear and courage and hope.

CHAPTER 19

Walking into her studio each morning, Rosie's fear would leave for a long coffee break, and working on the latest portrait, her courage would flit among her brushes like a hummingbird. Unfortunately, once home, her courage flitted away, and she did her best to distract her fear by watching silly soap operas. There was the girl in the hospital who has temporarily lost her sight from a hit-and-run, the man in prison accused of murder and blackmailing his attorney to defend him, and the two young kids in love and always kissing. Yuck.

Lou and Patty took turns checking in on her. As busy as they were growing their businesses, they'd often show up with dinner and hugs. Rosie loved seeing them, but after they left, she'd look at her crumbling life feeling empty and lost and not quite worthless but heading in that direction.

At the end of May, her brother invited her to come and meet the new foal he'd helped deliver two weeks earlier. She wasn't at all interested until Mark told her they'd stop at the Dairy Queen on the way back, a bribe that worked every time.

The next morning, he picked her up in his red Ford 150. After fifteen minutes west on blacktopped County Road E, they turned onto one side road and then another, and finally took a right onto a gravel drive where a sturdy sign on their left announced in large, deep blue letters that they'd arrived at Lily's Place, and the softly painted Monet-style lilies bordering the words made Rosie smile.

In fifty yards, they passed a small white farmhouse on the right with an inviting front porch. In another fifty yards, the gravel drive ended at a solid wooden barn. Next to it was an old weathered picnic table positioned near a gate to a fenced pasture and looking like an elderly security guard who had been on duty too long. Mark pulled in between a two-horse trailer and a pale green Chevy Silverado pickup.

Rosie turned to her brother. "I'm getting really nervous."

"I know. Since the horses are out in the pasture, let's walk through the empty barn first."

"Good plan. I don't understand how I can love painting horses when they scare me so much."

"One of life's many mysteries, I guess," Mark answered, hopping out of the truck while Rosie opened the passenger side door and cautiously slid her way out.

She'd been visiting other barns for her work and was familiar with, and enjoyed, the sweet smell of hay and earthy smell of leather.

"Check this out," Mark said as he opened a door and ushered Rosie into the barn office. Who knew a barn had an office? A battered desk with a swivel chair behind it occupied one side of the room with a metal file cabinet in the corner. On the desk, a large gray rock held a small stack of papers in place and an assortment of pens, pencils, and highlighters sprouted from a faded blue coffee mug. A worn sofa was pushed up against the wall across from the desk, and above it was a framed picture of horses grazing in a meadow.

"Mark?"

"Yes?"

"Mark!"

"Yes!"

"That's one of mine from high school."

"Indeed it is," he grinned. "When you started college you told me I could take one of your paintings, so I took one where you can actually see the horses' hooves."

"I'm a little embarrassed. It's not very good."

"Of course it is. Rosie, your talent is a gift. Accept it. Please. It's time."

"That's really hard for me to do."

"Well then," Mark said gently, "I suggest you practice," and not giving her a chance to respond, he announced, "Time to meet Markie."

"Who's Markie?"

"The new foal."

Rosie laughed. "Of course, it is."

Once at the pasture, She unenthusiastically stood by Mark as he leaned against the fence. Though Rosie did no leaning, she did appreciate the peaceful view. Blue sky. Green grass. Trees in the distance. Four horses calmly grazing while a curious, long-legged colt rushed around exploring his world.

"Markie is darling," said Rosie. "He reminds me of you when you were little."

"I will take that as a compliment."

"Good," she laughed. "That's how I meant it."

"Ah, thanks! Let me introduce you to the rest of the gang," and as if they were old friends, Mark told Rosie the names of each horse, which she immediately forgot.

"As an artist, you might want to know what the colors of their coats are called. The two brown ones with black manes and tails are called bay."

"Like a bay window?"

"Well, ah, sure," he sighed. "The one that looks more golden, Markie's mom, is called a chestnut."

"What's the gray called?"

"Gray."

"Ha!"

The chestnut mare had stopped grazing to carefully study Rosie from across the pasture and was now slowly walking toward her with Markie tagging along. Much to her surprise, Rosie didn't back away as the mare approached. This was a new mom after all, and something about that calmed her. When the mare got close enough, she stretched her neck over the fence and lowered her head so she could gently press it against Rosie's heart. Rosie's eyes immediately filled with tears. Timidly, she reached out and rested her hand on the mare's face. Neither moved until Markie whinnied for attention, and the mare carefully lifted her head, looking tenderly at Rosie before walking away.

Brother and sister walked slowly, almost reverently, to the picnic table. Mark told Rosie that she could come out to Lily's Place whenever she needed to get away. "Jill's the barn manager and lives in the farmhouse. I'll get you her number and let her know you'll be calling to set up a time to come again. Oh, and get yourself some work boots or find an old pair of shoes you don't mind ruining. It can get a little mucky around here."

Rosie looked down at her dusty, but not yet mucky, shoes and noticed a small black kitten under the picnic table who seemed to have been waiting patiently for her. Confidently, he rubbed up against her leg. She melted. He looked up at her with his big green eyes. She melted again. Bending down, she said, "I have to go now, but I look forward to seeing you again."

He blinked as if he understood, then ran to attack a random leaf skipping across the ground.

"Ready for that Dairy Queen now?"

Rosie looked up and grinned.

* * *

Three days later Mark was at her front door. In his arms was the green-eyed kitten. "Turns out this little guy had been abandoned, the older barn cats didn't want him around, and Jill said you could have him with her blessing. I've already taken him to the vet and had him checked out and made sure he got all his shots. Here's the vet's contact info, so when he's a bit older you can schedule a time for him to be neutered. I've got food and bowls, litter and a litter box, and lots of cat toys in my truck. Hold onto him while I bring it all in."

Rosie was stunned as Mark handed her the kitten who climbed right up onto her shoulder, put his nose into her neck, and began chewing on her hair.

Looking down at this sweet furry fellow, she wondered how she was going to take care of him when she could barely take care of herself.

Repositioning himself, the kitten curled up in her arms and shoved his nose into her armpit.

Okay, I guess we'll take care of each other.

"So, what'ya going to name him?" Mark asked after his last trip from the truck.

"Well, he's all black with no other markings so I could call him Spot."

"Very funny."

"Since we found him, or more accurately, he found us, by the picnic table, I think I'll call him Nick, well, Nicky. As in pic-nic-y. What'da think?"

"Love it! Well, gotta go. I'm off to another barn."

"Wait a minute. How can I thank you?"

He grinned and bopped her on the head. "No need, Rosie."

Not wanting to disturb the kitty in her arms, she didn't punch him back.

During the day, Nicky chased dust bunnies, wadded up paper, or anything else Rosie happened to drop. When he wore himself out, he'd simply collapse and fall asleep wherever he landed. Sitting on her lap in the evenings, he sometimes put his paw on her hand, and at night he curled up next to her when she went to sleep.

Nicky lifted Rosie's spirits enough that she began to venture out more often. Getting a little too cocky, she even RSVPed "yes" to a bridal shower luncheon that turned out to be not such a good idea. After that, Rosie decided she was done going out to anything remotely social. Until Patty called. She and Lou were having a couple of people over for dinner and asked if Rosie would join them and without thinking, she agreed.

"Wonderful!" Patty said. "It will be you, me, Lou, and two priests."

What?

CHAPTER 20

Rosie arrived Friday night at 7:00 p.m., not quite sure what to expect. When the door opened, her friends greeted her with hugs. Then Patty rushed back to the kitchen to check on things, and Lou introduced Rosie to Tom and John. Both looked to be in their early 80s. Tom's hair was white and still thick, while John was bald except for a white fringe around his head that looked like a halo had drifted down and settled there. Behind their glasses were wise, compassionate eyes. When they insisted they didn't want to be called Father, just Tom and John, she liked them immediately.

Over appetizers, they asked Rosie about herself. First, she told them she was an artist. Next, without knowing why, she confessed she was going through a difficult divorce. Do priests have that effect on people?

"I'm sorry for your pain," John said. "What is it you always say, Tom?"

"I always say, sometimes you just have to hang in there like a hair in a biscuit."

They smiled, and Rosie now knew where Patty had gotten that great line.

"And you're an artist. How wonderful," John said.

"I always say, the world needs creatives like you," Tom added.

When Patty announced that dinner was ready, they moved to the dining room table where waiting for them was a basket filled with still-warm, heavy-grained bread, cut into wedges. Rosie immediately took a piece. When it comes to warm bread, her manners went out the window. The meal, like the bread, was delicious, and the conversation was delightful. John told them about the time he worked on a cruise ship for a season and introduced himself as Father to the Catholics, Reverend to the Protestants, and Rabbi to the Jews. "I wasn't fooling anyone. On the contrary, they seemed to relax, appreciating that I was comfortable with whatever religion resonated with them. What is it you always say, Tom?"

"I always say that we are all connected and the essence of all religions is the same."

"Or should be," Patty inserted.

"Yes. Or should be," he sighed. "Anyway, the core message is that 'do unto others' piece which basically means be kind. When we can do that, as imperfectly as we might, we bring light and love into the world. Oh boy, here I go again, being sappy. It's an occupational hazard."

Lou then entered from the kitchen holding a tray with individual servings of dessert: warm apple crisp topped with a scoop of white chocolate gelato sprinkled with freshly ground nutmeg. Coffee was poured and after taking a sip, Rosie set down her cup and asked Tom and John if they had any advice about forgiveness, explaining that forgiving her soon-to-be ex was something she wasn't sure she'd ever be able to do. John reached across the table and patted her hand. "Don't worry about it, Rosie. You might not live long enough."

Rosie's mouth dropped open, and John asked Tom, "What is it you always say?"

"I always say that when you take the focus off the other person and instead focus on healing yourself, one day you'll notice that forgiveness has been a side effect of your healing."

John added, "Just like blooming flowers are a side effect of a gentle rain."

"Wow. Thanks."

"You're welcome. Are you going to finish your apple crisp?"

* * *

Rosie slept well that night, relieved that the forgiveness pressure was off. In the morning, she thought more about Tom and John's comments that kindness brings light and love into the world. That's a big deal. She hadn't thought of kindness that way, maybe because it's not boisterous and doesn't wear a flashy spandex outfit. She considered herself to be a kind person, well, except when it came to Ron. And except for the two Jehovah's Witnesses who rang her doorbell last Wednesday and to whom she rudely said, "No thanks," and slammed the door shut. Oops. And except for the driver who cut her off on the highway later that afternoon when she hollered, "Love and light to you, you miserable, thoughtless jerk." Later, it occurred to her that the driver might have been rushing to deal with an emergency, or if the driver was indeed a miserable, thoughtless jerk, he probably needed as much light and love as he could get.

"I could use some too," Rosie thought, but since she couldn't order them on Amazon, she supposed that meant it was up to her to bring them into her life. The first step, she thought, was that she'd have to be kinder to herself. How in the world would that work? Treating herself to chocolate and flowers seemed a little lame but couldn't hurt. Being in her studio was always good. She had a sense that spending time at Lily's Place had possibilities, but horses still made her uncomfortable. Maybe that's one of the places healing comes from, facing the uncomfortable, the things that frighten you, and finding the courage to let them rest in your arms as they transform…or you do.

What about accepting her confused, uncertain, mistake-riddled self with compassion? That would be the kindest of all, and the most difficult, and she wondered if that was even possible.

Rosie didn't run out to get chocolates or flowers, and accepting herself with compassion seemed too daunting a task. Instead, she called Jill, who suggested that she come out to the barn on Thursday morning, which turned out to be another lovely June day with blue skies and temperatures in the low 70s.

CHAPTER 21

When Rosie arrived, Jill was sitting on top of the picnic table, which looked more weathered than she remembered but much sturdier than she'd realized. She'd expected Jill to look weathered and sturdy as well, but she was petite, barely over five feet, with hazel eyes and short brown hair naturally high-lighted by the sun. Probably in her mid-thirties, wearing a faded tee shirt and jeans, Rosie marveled that she could handle four large horses, let alone a frisky colt.

After they both said how great it was to meet each other, Rosie thanked Jill for letting her come hang out, and Jill said anytime. Patting the top of the table, Jill invited Rosie to join her, which she did while holding onto the small tote she'd brought along and resting it next to her as if it was a very tiny third person. She'd packed the tote with a sketchbook and a few pencils. Keeping up with her portrait work had been a struggle, and she hoped that sketching in a fresh environment would reenergize her.

"This is a wonderful place to sit," Jill explained. "You can watch the horses and still keep your distance if you want."

Rosie nodded. "Keeping my distance sounds good. Other than taking pictures of them, I haven't been round horses much, and they make me nervous."

"I totally understand. They're big, and they move, but I have to say that surprises me. When I look at your painting hanging in the barn office, it feels like you truly have a connection with them."

Not knowing how to respond, Rosie said, "You must have spent a lot of time around horses."

"Yep. Starting in junior high I worked at a nearby hobby farm after school. The owners taught me a lot, paid me a little, and gave me free riding lessons."

"Did you ever fall off?"

"A few times. Gratefully never got hurt. I must bounce really well."

Rosie grinned. "How'd you end up here and basically running this place?"

"Well, it's something I never imagined I'd be doing, that's for sure. The owners, George and his wife Lily, are friends of my parents."

Ah, Rosie thought, the sign.

"They both really loved this place, and after deciding to retire to Florida, they didn't want to let the farm go. So, in exchange for caring for the horses, doing chores and up-keep, I live here rent free. Not only that, but they pay me. It's been wonderful. And, if something comes up, my buddy down the road comes to help out. Even better, it doesn't interfere with the history classes I teach at the U. It's an odd combination of jobs, I know, but it works for me."

"That's amazing. And why history?"

"History's always fascinated me. There's so much to learn from it, and the more you delve into it, the more you discover. I'm certain that if we paid more attention to our history, the world would be a better place." Jill chuckled. "That sounded like part of my introductory lecture."

"It's a wonderful answer."

"Thanks," Jill smiled. "Do you have any other questions?"

"Well, when my brother took me out here, he told me the names of each horse, but I can't remember any of them. Can you tell me again?"

"Sure. The gray is Harold. The bay with the snip of white on his nose is Clint. The bay with the white mark on his forehead that looks like a star is Shane. The chestnut is our new mom, Ginger, and her little one, of course, is Markie."

"How did they all end up here?"

"Clint was a racehorse who wasn't into running, Shane was on the rodeo circuit but wasn't into bucking, and Harold was a champion in endurance competitions but got badly injured. They all needed a home. Ginger most of all. She was found abandoned and pregnant."

"I had no idea."

"They're what makes this place so special—and why I love working here."

"It feels special to me, too, and I can't believe I'm saying this, but if it's all right with you, I'd like to make Thursday mornings a regular thing."

"Absolutely. I'd love it. I need to finish some chores now, but stay as long as you like and if you think of it, come say goodbye before you leave."

"Thanks, I will."

Smiling, Jill hopped off the table and headed for the barn.

* * *

Watching the small herd, it didn't take long for Rosie to see that Shane was shy, Clint was bossy, dear Harold was the peacekeeper, and all three kept a watchful eye on Ginger and Markie. As they grazed, Rosie felt an unexpected sense of wonder. She'd always assumed wonder was about looking at skies filled with stars or soaring mountains or boundless oceans, especially at sunset, but sometimes wonder is right in front of you. It's hard to find in the midst of grief, and Rosie was grateful it had appeared this Thursday morning. She sat for thirty minutes with wonder warming her like the June sun, then left with her tote unopened.

The following Thursday, after a short picnic table visit with Jill, Rosie was sitting alone and cautiously opened her tote, resurrecting her sketchbook as if it was a relic from a distant past. A treasure that had been lost and rediscovered. Treasure though it might have been, it was quite bossy and hollered at her. "Get back to work!"

"Okay, okay," she mumbled and began to draw. Finishing each sketch, she'd quickly turn the page and started another so she'd have no time to study what she'd done and judge it, which helped her to be freer as she worked. She sketched the distant trees, the weathered fencing around the pasture, the side of the barn and, of course, the horses. She even sketched the patterns in the weathered wood of the picnic table.

Once home, she took a deep breath before looking at her work. Not to her surprise, some sketches were terrible. Yet, some were okay, and there were one or two that, dare she say it, were pretty darn good. Rosie was feeling something she hadn't felt in a long time. Joy.

* * *

Over the next couple of weeks with Jill's encouragement, Rosie began bringing treats for the horses. Before sitting on the picnic table to draw, she'd stand on her side of the fence and reach her arm over it with pieces of apples or carrots in the palm of her open hand. As she got braver, she'd walk into the pasture to give them out. Before long, she was rubbing the horses' necks, and they in turn nuzzled her shoulders. They had become an unexpected support system for Rosie, a gift found in something she had once feared.

Soon, Jill and Rosie's picnic table meetings skipped right over the superficial. The women talked, instead, about the emotions that came with life transitions and things falling apart and coming back together in unexpected ways, and about why relationships did or didn't work. Jill knew Rosie was going through a divorce and shared that she was never married but had been in a relationship for eight years that ended quite badly.

"Recognizing, and admitting, the truth about a broken relationship is hard," she said, "Sometimes the truth saves us, but it has a tendency to wander off when no one wants to hear it, and it's up to us to save the truth before it gets lost in a forest or falls off a cliff or drowns in a river."

Rosie nodded in agreement, and they both sat quietly with their own private thoughts.

* * *

The first time Jill invited Rosie into the farmhouse was for cold lemonade on an oppressively hot morning. They entered through the side door and into a mud room. Jill explained, "This is where anyone who has been hanging out in the barn area takes off their shoes or boots before going anywhere else."

Jill kicked hers off. Rosie, with her newly purchased boots, did the same and followed Jill down a short hallway past a laundry room, bathroom, and around a corner into a bright, updated, and efficiently compact kitchen.

Past the kitchen was a heavy wooden dining room table, and past that the hardwood floors were covered with an area rug on which a sofa and two chairs faced a fireplace. The front door and two windows were on the right of the room and a staircase to the second floor on the left.

"Welcome to my home, sweet home."

"Jill, your home is simply wonderful."

"Thanks," she grinned, "I think so, too, and check this out." Rosie followed Jill to a hallway she hadn't noticed that turned to run along the back of the house and where Jill's bedroom, office, and bathroom were located.

"I have to tell you, I love this place," declared Rosie.

"Me too. Now, I'll get the lemonade and some of my homemade chocolate brownies, and we'll sit down and solve the problems of the world."

CHAPTER 22

Going inside for lemonade became a new, refreshing summer routine, and the chocolate brownies were always a treat. Solving the problems of the world, not so much. Too many people were not paying attention to history.

Two weeks later, Rosie mentioned that their house had sold faster than expected, and she'd been looking for apartments to rent but hadn't yet found one that felt right.

Jill slowly nodded. "Come upstairs with me. There's something I want to show you."

The second floor was larger than Rosie imagined. On her left was an open space filled with light from an over-sized window. On her right were two bedrooms with a linen closet and an updated bathroom between them.

"This is amazing."

"I think so, too. This space was originally created for Lily and George's adult children when they'd visit from out of town, but now they visit their parents in Florida. And, I have a question for you. How about moving in here? You'd have the entire floor to yourself and could use one of the rooms as your studio, plus there's the mini-living room, sitting area, whatever you want to call it, with a great view, where you could hang out when you wanted to be alone. What'da think?"

"What did you say?"

Jill smiled. "Ah, you heard me."

"I have to sit down," Rosie said as she sank onto the hardwood floor.

Jill sat down next to her and patted her knee.

"I'm overwhelmed and think I might cry. I don't know what to say. That's not true. You have no idea how much I want to say yes, but are you sure? You barely know me."

"Oh, I can tell a lot about someone by how they inter-act with horses and how horses respond to them. They're usually a better judge of character than I am."

"This offer is so thoughtful, so generous, and again, I'm truly overwhelmed and don't know if I can think clearly. Can I have a couple of friends come over to check things out and talk it through with me to make sure I'm not doing something rash?"

"Of course. Wise idea."

"Before I get too carried away, what about rent? How much are you thinking?"

"Well, if you help me with a few daily chores when you can, and if I get first dibs and discounts on any paintings you put up for sale, there's no rent. And, I don't want you to feel any pressure. If at any time you sense it's not working out, you can leave, and if I ever feel that way, I'll tell you to leave. How does that sound?"

"Sounds fair to me."

"Just so you know, this isn't as spontaneous as you may think. It's been on my mind for a while. You'll have your own safe space but won't feel like you're alone."

Rosie whispered, "Thank you."

* * *

By the time she was back at her house, Rosie'd already decided which room would be her bedroom and which would be the studio and how she'd arrange each of them. Calling Lou, words tumbled out of her like popcorn spilling across a kitchen floor. Laughing, Lou said she'd get back to her with the day and time that worked best.

Rosie called her attorney to make sure that moving out of the house wouldn't affect her divorce settlement, and it wouldn't. She left a message on David's answering machine explaining her potential move and asking if there was anything he wanted from the house that she could keep for him, which he didn't.

The thought of traveling light was very appealing to Rosie. Except for a few sentimental things, Rosie really didn't want to take much. There were the items that had been discussed with attorneys and agreed on that included half the kitchen contents and linens, a dresser, a bookcase, some books, two mismatched end tables, the bed, and two framed prints that she loved and Ron never really cared for. So much for traveling light.

Lou called back to say that she and Patty would pick her up Sunday at 10:00 a.m. Rosie confirmed things with Jill and then collapsed onto the sofa and closed her eyes.

* * *

Lou and Patty not only picked up Rosie but picked up lunch as well. When they pulled onto the gravel drive, Lou looked at the sign. "That reminds me of the picture of the lilies above your parents' fireplace."

"I know. Me too. Do you think it's a 'sign'?"

"Well," Patty huffed, "it's definitely a sign."

Jill welcomed everyone. "It's so thoughtful of you to bring lunch. If you need to put anything in the fridge, be my guest. I'm off to do some paperwork in the barn office so you'll have privacy to look around. I also left a folder on the table with info about the updated plumbing, electrical, and gas."

After examining the farmhouse from top to bottom with Rosie tagging along behind them, Patty announced, "I wouldn't change a thing. I say go for it."

Lou agreed. "This place feels like a magical and extraordinary gift."

Patty rolled her eyes at the word magical and asked, "How about a magical lunch?"

While Lou and Patty were setting the table, Rosie retrieved Jill from the barn office. Celebrating over a giant chef salad, fresh fruit, and Jill's chocolate brownies, they decided Rosie would move into the farmhouse in two weeks.

* * *

Staggering from the speed of this move, Rosie began packing up boxes and making a few trips to the farm, where she hung clothes in her new closet and placed a set of sheets and a towel in the linen closet. On the floor of her bedroom, she set down two boxes of clothes that would go into her dresser and a box of books for the bookcase. She left the box of kitchen items downstairs for Jill to look through in case there was anything she might want.

On her last night in the house where she'd lived for over twenty years, Rosie was physically and emotionally exhausted but couldn't sleep. Thoughts always got darker for her in the middle of the night. What was she doing? What was she thinking? Would this be another huge mistake?

On moving day, she'd planned to get to the farmhouse by 8:00 a.m., and since Patty's movers weren't available until early afternoon, Rosie'd given her a spare key. It took her longer than she thought to finish packing the car. After saving room for the cat carrier and everything else that would come with Nicky, there was no room left for the two framed prints, and she placed them in the entryway so the movers wouldn't miss them. It was closer to 10:00 when, with her purse over her shoulder and holding the carrier with a very vocal Nicky inside it, Rosie walked out of the house for the last time. She left without tears, only a profound sadness for what could have been mixed with tremendous relief.

* * *

Arriving at what would now be her new home, it took a few trips up the stairs to get Nicky and his food, water, litter, and favorite toys into the soon-to-be studio. As she unzipped the carrier, he stared at her, making it quite clear that he planned on staying right where he was.

"It's okay, Nicky. You'll just have to stay in this room until things are moved in and have calmed down. You're safe. You're safe," she repeated a few more times, reassuring herself more than him. Leaving the room, Rosie softly closed the door behind her and went to her car, making a few more trips up the stairs with random boxes. On her last trip she gently carried her grandmother's quilt into her bedroom. To keep it safe for the day, she placed it on the closet shelf.

Back downstairs, she noticed a note from Jill on the dining room table saying she was out running errands and

Rosie should help herself to the fresh coffee, which she did immediately. Carrying her cup to the dining room table, she sat and stared at nothing. Then she moved to a chair facing the fireplace and stared at the picture above it with a bridge disappearing into a mist, then moved again to the front porch to do more staring.

"Enough already with the staring," she said out loud, sounding like her grandmother, which got Rosie's attention. She quickly stood, got into her car, drove to the grocery store, and stocked up on food to contribute to her new household. After returning and putting away her purchases, she made and enjoyed a grilled cheese sandwich, after which she walked to the picnic table and sat watching the horses and remembering their stories. Ginger had been abandoned. Harold had been badly injured. Clint and Shane had reached a point when what was expected of them, whether it was racing or bucking, was no longer what they expected or wanted for themselves. All had found healing at Lily's Place, a place where Rosie hoped to find the same. She sent a silent thank you to this four-legged community of survivors. Knowing this was where she belonged, Rosie found a deep sense of peace and hoped it would reappear whenever she needed. She hadn't considered peace was always with her, underneath all the noise, singing its sweet melody.

CHAPTER 23

Rosie was still sitting on the picnic table when the caravan arrived. The mover's truck was in the lead, followed by Lou, with Patty in her car. With impeccable timing, Mark followed in his truck, and less than five minutes later, their folks arrived with Aunt Sophie in the back seat.

Rosie hugged everyone except for Aunt Sophie, who stared blankly back at her, daring her to approach, and she couldn't get near Patty, who was supervising the movers. The first thing out of the truck was a new bed.

"That goes upstairs into the larger bedroom," Patty told them.

"Wait. What's this?" asked a startled Rosie.

"You didn't expect me to let you sleep in your old bed, did you?" Patty yelled from the truck.

"Well, I…."

"No need to answer. It was a rhetorical question." Before turning back to her supervising, she added, "By the way, the movers told me they looked everywhere, but the two framed pictures weren't in the house."

"Argh! There's only one way they could have disappeared. I'll have Cynthia call Ron's attorney in the morning."

Rosie went inside and watched as her bookshelf and one of the end tables joined her new bed. A soft blue chair that Rosie'd never seen before was also placed in the room, and its matching sofa was settled into the sitting area alongside the second end table.

Mark and his dad each carried a large plastic bag up the steps, then quickly retreated back down the stairs and out onto the porch. Aunt Sophie and her Camels had already claimed a chair where she could smoke in peace. Nodding at her, they wisely sat as far away as possible.

"Looks like my little girl has done good," said his dad.

"Yep."

"I was worried."

"I know."

They both nodded, looking at the sky as if it held answers to the mysteries of the universe.

Back upstairs, Lou and Rosie's mom were putting freshly laundered sheets on the bed as well as a new comforter. Before Rosie could speak, her mom kissed her on the cheek and said, "The new things you didn't expect are gifts from your father and me, and all you have to say is thanks," and Rosie did.

Her mom filled the linen closet with another set of sheets and a set of towels, along with a few scented soaps and lotions, all of which came from the bags her brother and dad had dropped in the hallway. Back in the bedroom, Lou filled the bookcase, Rosie filled the dresser, and as a finishing touch, removed her grandmother's quilt from the closet shelf for the last time and tenderly placed it across the back of the soft blue chair.

With their work done, the three of them came down the stairs just as Aunt Sophie was about to rearrange the living room furniture. Apparently, she had gotten bored on the porch and was looking for a creative outlet. Rosie guided her back outside, and Mark took the opportunity to invite everyone to meet the horses, which they thoroughly enjoyed. Returning to the farmhouse, they watched as another car pulled into the driveway, and a tall, good-looking young man with soft brown hair and big brown eyes got out.

"David!" Rosie screamed and ran to her son. They hugged, separated, looked at each other, and hugged again.

"You look wonderful," she said.

"I am. You look tired."

"I am."

By then everyone had gathered around them. There was a whirlwind of hugs and kisses and questions flying through the air like a swarm of hungry summer mosquitoes. "How was your drive?" "How's teaching?" "Are you hungry?"

"Of course he's hungry," her mom said, pulling him into the house and quickly introducing him to Jill, who had just returned with dinner from a local barbecue place and announced, "Your Early Bird Special is now being served."

Sitting down, Rosie asked, "Did you all know that David was coming?"

"Of course we did!" they cheered, and she laughed.

Her mom must have been tired because she never asked if Rosie wanted more of anything, but Rosie was quite disturbed when she caught herself turning to David and about to ask, "More chicken?"

Patty stood and presented Rosie with a "welcome to your new home" card signed by everyone and a gift certificate for The Artists Supply Shop. Next, Aunt Sophie stood to give a toast, her face softening as she began.

"Listen to your dreams. They will reveal to you the roads you are meant to travel. Listen to your heart. It will tell you all you need to know. Listen to your fear without judgment. It will be calmed by your compassion."

There was a moment of stunned silence, and then Aunt Sophie was applauded, which made her quite uncomfortable. Her sour face returned, and she sat down with a thunk. They'd glimpsed a tender part of her, and it made Rosie sad to wonder why she chose to hide it so well.

After dinner, Rosie excused herself from helping to clean up and instead led David up the stairs. "Check this out," she said, eager to know what he would think.

Carefully looking around, he couldn't stop smiling. "It's really fabulous, Mom. I'm so excited for you."

"Thanks honey. Me too."

"What's with the closed door? Is that where your studio will be?"

"Yep, I was going to show that to you next, because it's also where I put Nicky until the commotion of the day was over."

"Wise decision. I haven't seen him since the last time I came home."

"Come say hello. He loves you."

"The feeling is mutual."

Rosie cautiously opened the door to make sure Nicky didn't scoot out, but she didn't have to worry. He was resting contentedly on a windowsill, and it wasn't until David sat on the floor and said, "Hey, Nicky, how're you doin'," that he jumped down, walked over, rubbed against David, and curled up in his lap purring.

Rosie sat down next to her son. "I have something important to tell you that I haven't shared with anyone else yet."

David stopped petting Nicky and seriously focused on his mother.

"You know my grandmother's maiden name was Hope, right?"

He nodded.

"I've always loved that. A simple word, yet filled with such possibilities. After a lot of thought, I've decided to take that as my last name, and next week I'll be starting the process to make it official."

With a relieved laugh, he leaned over and hugged her. "Mom, I think it's a beautiful idea. It's not the name that binds us together anyway. I'm just grateful you're not changing it to She Who Mucks Out Stalls."

"Aaww. That was my second choice."

* * *

By the time they came back downstairs, not only was the kitchen clean, but Jill and Mark had already brought the horses back into the barn and fed them. A half-hour later, Mark left, followed by their folks with Aunt Sophie, who nodded at Rosie as they pulled away. When Rosie walked David to his car, he told her that he'd be staying overnight with friends, having breakfast with his dad in the morning, and wanted to have lunch with her before he drove back to Madison.

"Of course, of course," she said, blinking away tears, and after one more hug, letting him go on his way.

Lou and Patty were the last to leave, but not before informing Rosie they'd be helping her pack up her studio the next Saturday.

Worn out, the two new housemates went inside and shared a final hug for the evening. Jill went to her room, and Rosie went upstairs to her new space, life, home. She wasn't sure what to call it. Opening her soon-to-be studio door, she found Nicky back on the windowsill. His new circumstances didn't seem to bother him all that much. Seeing her, he jumped down, and after rubbing against her leg, walked calmly across the landing, stopping for a moment to look at the stairs and where they disappeared into the darkness. Not that impressed, he followed Rosie into her bedroom. When she got into bed, so did he, claiming a spot next to her pillow. In a few minutes, they were both gently snoring. The next morning Rosie woke with Nicky asleep on her chest, feeling his soft purr against her heart.

* * *

Jill was making coffee when Rosie came downstairs and surprised her with a framed sketch she'd done of Markie asleep in the pasture. Jill grinned and surprised Rosie with a framed print of Georgia O'Keeffe's *The Ladder*, which was filled with powerful images of transitions. Laughing, they rushed to help each other hang pictures, and after a quick cup of coffee, they were off to do chores.

As Jill opened the front door, Nicky walked down the stairs like royalty.

Living with Rosie, he'd become an indoor cat, and she worried that if he got the chance, he'd dash outside at any opportunity. Nicky noticed the open door but looked away from it with a haughty attitude. It was quite clear that going outside was beneath him, and he'd rather find adventures in this safe, new territory.

Rosie found herself in new territory, as well, the moment she and Jill walked into the barn that morning. Apparently, this was the cue for whinnying and hoof stomping to begin. The horses acted like rude restaurant customers demanding their food immediately or surely they would collapse from hunger. Jill smiled, telling Rosie not to be concerned; it was just part of the morning routine.

With a little coaching from her, the two of them made a good team. Jill fed the horses and Rosie watered them. While they were chowing down, Jill repaired a small section of the fencing while Rosie refilled the outdoor water trough. Then Jill let the horses out into the pasture, and together she and Rosie mucked out the stalls as David predicted she would. It turned out Rosie was a wiz at mucking. Go figure. Chores done, they returned to the farmhouse where Jill went to work on lesson plans for her history classes, and Rosie went upstairs. Laying down on her bed, she fell asleep for two hours. All that fresh air can really knock a girl out.

The late afternoon chores took less time, and Rosie found she actually enjoyed the work. It was like cleaning up after a bunch of teenagers but with less attitude. By the end of the first week, she felt physically stronger and mentally calmer.

CHAPTER 24

No chores for Rosie on Saturday. It was studio moving day, and she woke early feeling like a six-year-old who could hardly wait to see what Santa left under the tree. Well, being Jewish, it was how she assumed a six-year-old would feel. Arriving at the Uniroyal Building fifteen minutes before Lou and Patty, she unlocked the warehouse door, walked down the hall, unlocked her studio door, swung it open, and froze. Everything was gone. This sacred space where she felt safe, where she worked and created, this space that was witness to her joy, frustration, and determination, was empty.

When Lou and Patty found Rosie, she was sitting on the floor, in a corner, knees up to her chin, and arms wrapped around her legs, staring at the painting of the red balloon, that for some reason had been left hanging on the wall across from her. Lou immediately sat down next to her, putting her arm around Rosie's shoulders. Patty swore loudly and ran to find the building manager who lived in an apartment on the second floor. She returned, dragging behind her a thin man with thin lips and thin hair, wearing a T-shirt, jeans, and slippers.

"What's the problem here? I got your letter saying that you would be moving out a few days earlier than expected."

"You got a letter?" Patty asked with controlled rage.

"Sure. It's in my files."

"Get it. Right. Now," she demanded.

Baffled, he rushed out, returning in less than five minutes with the letter that Patty immediately grabbed out of his hand. It was typed, but there was a signature at the bottom. Kneeling beside Rosie, she asked, "Is this your signature?"

Looking up, Rosie shook her head "no."

Lou looked at the letter and agreed.

The manager was shocked. "Oh, I'm so sorry. I had no way of knowing." His concern and empathy was quite large, not thin at all.

Patty was stunned, "Oh my God, could Ron have done this?"

Rosie quietly answered. "I believe he did. Yes."

Lou stood and calmly spoke to the manager. "Thank you for your help. Can we use your phone? You're not in any trouble, but we have to contact her attorney immediately."

"Absolutely. Again, I'm so sorry. I can't believe this happened."

"Rosie, sweetie, you've got to get up so you can call your attorney, and we need to do that right now."

With her friends' support, Rosie carefully stood, then walked a bit unsteadily across the room to her balloon painting. Lifting it off the wall, she held it close, like the promise it was, the promise that could have disappeared but miraculously remained. Then she walked out of the room and did not look back.

* * *

Rosie's attorney, Cynthia, had been spending her Saturday morning catching up with office work and answered the phone after three rings. Tough, compassionate, and practical, she carefully listened as Rosie explained what had happened and her belief that Ron emptied the studio, saying, "He's been trying to separate me from my art for years."

"Rosie, I'm so sorry. I can't imagine how you must feel. It's important that I ask you a few questions now. Are you okay with that?"

"Yes."

"Good. First, I will need that letter. If you're able to get it to my office this morning, I'll be here for another hour."

Rosie looked at Lou and Patty, who had been hovering. They nodded, and Rosie answered, "That will work."

"Great. Now, what was the dollar value of everything that was taken?"

"Oh, but Cynthia, it's more than the dollar value. It's like he took a part of my heart," her voice cracked as a sob tried to escape.

"I know, and I understand. But as your attorney, I have to ask, because my next question will be, do you want to spend a lot more money on my legal fees to prove it was Ron, or would you rather spend considerably less money to replace what was taken, start fresh, and not drag out the emotional pain any longer than you have to. Proving Ron did this can be done but will be quite expensive, and I don't want to bill you for something that will not benefit you all that much in the end. Take time to think about this before you give me an answer. Meanwhile, I'll share what you've told me with Ron's attorney, and since we've already advised him of the two disappearing prints, it may encourage them to settle more quickly and with terms more beneficial to you. Again, take your time. I'm sure you're in shock right now."

"I must be. I feel mostly flat, but as soon as I'm able, I'll get back to you with my decision as well as with the itemized value of what was taken."

"Sounds good, and most importantly, please take good care of yourself."

Before Rosie could respond, Patty grabbed the phone. "Give me your office address, and we'll be on our way with the letter."

Lou thanked the kindhearted manager, and Patty drove the three of them directly to the attorney's office, insisting Rosie and Lou wait by the car while she ran into the building to drop off the letter along with the manager's name and contact information. Mission accomplished, the three of them walked slowly down the block and around the corner to a cafe.

"You need to eat something," Lou said as they sat down.

"I don't think I can."

"Just coffee, then?"

Rosie nodded.

When it arrived, she looked at her friends. "I don't know how I would have gotten through this morning without you both. Thank you from the bottom of my heart."

They each took one of her hands and squeezed.

"I've been trying to think why he would do such a thing. Does he feel like he's losing control, and this was a tantrum to prove that he's not—and that at least in his mind, he's now won." Rosie shook her head. "He still always needs to win." She turned into herself as if searching for something. Answers. Truths. A way forward.

Her friends waited silently until Rosie returned from wherever she had gone and abruptly said, "I'm going to make up my own mind about the two options Cynthia shared, but I really want to hear your thoughts."

"This is a decision you need to make on your own," said Patty. "Just make sure it's in *your* best interest and know that whatever you decide, we'll support you."

"Well, my best interest would be that I have a better divorce settlement," Rosie said. "I'm desperate not to be a victim but don't know if that's possible right now. I've been trying to reclaim myself, but it's incredibly hard and doesn't seem to be working out."

"Speaking of reclaiming," Lou said, "or should I say replacing. How about going to The Artists Supply Shop and getting you some fresh supplies? We can use your coupon."

"I don't have it with me."

"Not a problem. They'll have a record of it."

Rosie answered with a noncommittal, "Okay."

Patty dropped Lou and Rosie back at the warehouse and drove away. Lou took Rosie's car keys, unlocked the doors, and settled into the driver's seat, "Consider me your chauffeur for the afternoon."

Before they'd left for the attorney's office, Rosie had carefully placed her balloon painting on the floor behind the passenger seat, and only after checking on it did she get into the car. While Lou drove, she closed her eyes, thinking about another decision she needed to make. Did she want to be miserable that she had to start all over again, or did she want to be grateful she was able to start again? Sounds like an easy choice, but right now she wanted to be miserable.

* * *

Rosie loved art supply stores even more than bookstores, and her energy rallied for a short time. When the shopping was finished and their purchases in the car trunk, they headed back to Lily's Place, where Patty was waiting for them on the front porch. She and Lou unloaded the car, while Rosie carried her precious painting up the steps and into the studio, leaned it against the wall and sat down next to it, drained.

Patty spread a drop cloth across the floor and, standing in the doorway, bragged, "I think this looks particularly good, if I do say so myself." Then she and Lou set up the easel, put brushes and paints on the small rolling cabinet, and canvases in the closet. Lou even found a nail and hammer, and soon the balloon had a special place on the wall of its new home.

Doing her best to smile, Rosie said, "You guys did it again, and it's a good thing we're close friends because I'm going to have a seriously ugly, snot-running, hiccupping cry."

Lou grabbed a fresh box of tissues for her from the bathroom, and after Rosie's tears stopped flowing, she blew her nose so loudly it was like a trumpet announcing Jill's arrival. She appeared with a bag full of Sammie's subs in one hand and in the other was a heavier bag of cold Cokes, Diet Cokes, and Dr Peppers. Lou and Patty helped her unload everything onto the drop cloth. Jill sat down next to Rosie, giving her a hug and explaining that Patty had already shared what happened.

About to take a bite of her turkey sub, Rosie changed her mind and set it down. "I have something I'm embarrassed and ashamed to say." Looking at her friends, she took a deep breath, squeezed her eyes shut, and wailed, "I hate him I hate him I hate him I hate him." Pausing to take another breath, she repeated, "I hate him I hate him I hate him."

There was a brief silence. Then Patty said, "Sounds like the nice girl has just left the building."

"I don't want to feel this way. It's scaring me. I feel like I'm turning into…argh, I don't know what I'm turning into."

Always practical, Patty said, "The issue isn't the rage and anger. It's what you do with the tremendous energy of these feelings that will matter."

Jill added, "Let me share something with you that I learned from Mark. It might not make sense right away, but stay with me. A couple years ago, when I was taking the horses in from the pasture one afternoon, I noticed that Harold had gotten a puncture wound on his leg. How that happened I never figured out. Anyway, it was very deep. I cleaned it out the best I could and covered it with a leg wrap. When I checked on him the next morning, his leg had swollen up so much that I was really worried and called Mark to come out and take a look. He explained that I shouldn't have covered it, and it's often better to keep deep wounds open to let any infection drain. He explained it was going to look really nasty as all the infection from the wound oozed out, but that was the only way for it to heal. You, dear Rosie, have been wounded very deeply, so don't try to cover up those feelings, even though when they leak out, they're going to be hard to deal with."

"That's quite a visual, but I understand. I can't say that some of my anger won't leak out and splatter all over Ron, at least for a while, and thank you all for listening. I feel better admitting this, and it's kept my head from exploding."

* * *

The next morning, knowing it was not a wise decision, she picked up the phone and called Ron anyway. What was she doing? Why did she call? Simple. She wanted answers. Hearing his voice was painful. It was a voice she once loved to hear. But no more.

"I know what you did and didn't know you could be so cruel. I want to know why. Why?"

He paused, and his pause said it all. Still, he answered with, "I don't know what you're talking about."

Her anger didn't just leak out. It shot up like Old Faithful as she yelled, "You certainly do!" and slammed down the receiver. "What did I expect him to say?" she mumbled. "This 'using energy wisely' thing is going to take a lot of practice."

CHAPTER 25

September arrived crisp and cool. Sitting on the picnic table after morning chores, Rosie asked Jill, "So, how're your lesson plans going for the fall semester?"

"They're pretty much done, which is always a relief. How about you? How's the painting coming?"

"Tough question. I'm really frustrated. I can't quite get started and just keep rearranging things, but there're only so many ways to organize tubes of paint."

"What do you think's holding you back?"

"I've been asking myself that same question. I think it's the persistent feeling that I'm not good enough mixed with the fear that once I start, someone will try to take it all away from me again."

"I'm so sorry. Can I offer a suggestion?"

"Sure."

"Have you ever considered painting your fear? I have a feeling you'll find some answers. And if that helps, you may want to consider painting your tears as well."

Astonished by this insightfully simple suggestion, Rosie stared at Jill, who patted her on the shoulder and hopped off the picnic table to give Rosie time to consider. And consider she did.

Within minutes, she was in her studio with a blank canvas on her easel and fresh paints on her palette. There is power in beginning—and excitement. There is also anxiety and the urge to change your mind and go organize your sock drawer, which Rosie was considering until she mentally slapped herself and went to work. Her first brush strokes were timid, her colors drab and muted, but it didn't take long for her to let go, get bolder, braver. She painted her fear in dark shadows with sharp red slashing lines like lava escaping from a volcano as her fear turned to anger and then grief.

On a second canvas, she painted her tears tumbling down like a waterfall, each one carrying within it a soft, beautiful reflection of light.

Once finished, Rosie was worn out but felt a weight had lifted off her shoulders. She wasn't sure if she'd found answers, but she'd made a decision. She was no longer going to focus on what was holding her back but on what was lovingly propelling her forward. "Ah, much better," she thought. Since it was almost dinner time and she hadn't eaten since breakfast, she went down to the kitchen. Opening the refrigerator, she took out a cold Dr Pepper and the turkey sub she'd picked up the day before.

Turkey was now her favorite sub. A mound of chips completed the dinner that soon revived her, and Rosie was confident that she wouldn't be organizing her sock drawer anytime soon.

Since the divorce had started, Rosie stopped taking on any additional horse portraits, but the next morning she called the potential clients who had been on her waiting list. She thanked them for their patience and asked to schedule a time to meet at their barns and take pictures of their horses. A few had changed their minds, but six were thrilled and looking forward to seeing her. Next she called Patty and shared the results of her efforts. "Could this be the beginning of a viable business?"

"Rosie, your business motor has been idling for quite a while, waiting for you to climb into the driver's seat and put it in gear. So yes. Now, listen up. You need to charge much more for your portraits. They are worth it. And, remember, take time to paint other subjects that inspire or intrigue you. I have no doubt that galleries would want to offer them for sale and so would I, and I'll gladly make prints of them again, with your permission, of course. Now, this is your business, not mine, so do whatever feels right. I'm well aware that I can be bossy and have a tendency to get carried away. Am I overwhelming you?"

"I don't think so."

"Okay. One more thing. Whenever you start to doubt yourself, you call me. Is that clear?"

"Clear. And thank you."

* * *

By the end of the month, Rosie had completed two commissioned portraits, leaves were turning red and gold, and the divorce had settled quickly, just as Rosie's attorney had said it would. The last day of the month was Rosh Hashanah, the Jewish New Year, which Rosie felt was quite appropriate.

Her parents were once again hosting the holiday dinner. It was a smaller gathering this time with her, Mark and his family, and Aunt Sophie. Greeting Rosie at the door, her mom gave her a big hug. "I'm so grateful that your divorce is over." Letting go of her daughter, she added, "probably not as grateful as you. You must feel so much better."

"I wish. The divorce papers may be signed, but the feeling better part is going to take a while."

Her mom looked a little deflated, and Rosie gave her a kiss on the cheek just as her dad appeared, patted her on the shoulder, looked at his wife and said, "Let's eat."

There was no chicken soup or bouncing matzah balls, but there was still brisket and the familiar side dishes. It wasn't until dessert that the traditional questioning began. "Chocolate cake?" "Apple pie?" "A little of both?"

Rosie smiled and shook her head "no" with each offer, comforted that there were still things she could depend on to be constant in her life.

At the end of the evening, as she was about to leave, her mom pulled her aside. "I have a friend who has a son, and well," she hesitated, "well, we thought it would be nice for the two of you to get together for coffee."

"Oh Mom, no. No, no, noooo!"

"Could I bribe you with a Dairy Queen?"

"Trust me, Mom, a Dairy Queen won't do it."

Not one to give up, her mom tried again. "Okay, how about this. I won't ask you if you want more of anything at the end of a meal for…hummm…how about six months?"

They both laughed, and Rosie gave in.

"Wonderful! I'll tell his mother to have Ted call you. That's his name, Ted."

Rosie kissed her mom good-bye and walked out the door. It's only for coffee, she thought, and she did have a lovely time visiting with the priests at Lou and Patty's, so how bad could it be.

The next morning, instead of dressing up for services at the synagogue, Rosie put on jeans and a sweatshirt. She walked along the outside of the pasture fence to the far end and laid down on her back in the shade of a large oak tree, feeling the earth strong and solid and a bit lumpy beneath her. Looking up, she saw sunlight sparkle around the edges of the leaves as they fluttered in the gentle breeze. When the wind gusted and the branches swayed, the leaves revealed a brilliant blue sky. Rosie wondered what she would see in the new year when the winds blew through her life and hoped she'd remember there was an infinite sky above during the times she couldn't see it.

Ten days after Rosh Hashanah was Yom Kippur. The Day of Atonement and fasting.

Since she was thirteen years old, Rosie had always fasted. This year she started out to do the same until 2:00 p.m., when she sat down at the kitchen table with a container of yogurt, feeling guilty with each spoonful she swallowed. "What kind of person am I, eating on Yom Kippur?"

She followed the yogurt with a piece toast and continued to worry. "What's happening? Am I weak? Selfish? Will there be cosmic punishment involved?"

Wait a minute! What kind of a God would punish me for eating a container of yogurt and a piece of toast? Who would create that kind of God in the first place? I don't want a religion that bullies me. Doing things because you feel threatened is not faith.

Having resolved this issue, the question of forgiveness was next, because Yom Kippur was also a day to ask for, and to offer, forgiveness. But since this was something Rosie was still working on, she simply went up to her room, covered herself with her grandmother's quilt, and laid down.

CHAPTER 26

osie and Ted agreed to meet at the Caribou Coffee shop at 10:00 the following Tuesday. She also agreed to meet Lou at Embers at 11:30 for a debriefing. Rosie arrived a few minutes early, got her coffee, and sat down at a table. She was nervous until she saw a man come in, walk right past her, and make a beeline for the young, blond, curvy woman waiting for her order.

When the woman shook her head no, the man turned and noticed Rosie, and she thought, "Oh boy, here we go."

Ted walked over and introduced himself, then got his coffee, returned, and sat down. His hair was dark brown, his eyes blue. He seemed a little too cocky and like he enjoyed working out a little too much. Rosie nodded as he talked for the next thirty minutes about how successful he was as a CPA and about his many trips. Mexico. France. Italy. Spain. Transitioning to sports, he decided to add Rosie to the conversation, even though he was doing just fine by himself.

"Tennis. Do you play tennis?" he asked.

"No"

"Golf. Do you play golf?"

"No"

"Oh, I bet you bike. Do you bike?"

"No."

Ted didn't give up. He continued the interrogation, asking if she hiked or jogged or worked out at a gym. Rosie considered telling him she mucked out stalls for exercise but assumed that would only confuse him.

He finally asked, "So what do you do?"

"I'm an artist."

"Oh, so you don't bike?"

By then it was 11:00, and she'd had enough. Trying not to be rude, she explained that she had to get to another meeting. He didn't seem disappointed that she was leaving, which made sense since, after all, she didn't bike.

Rosie was already seated in a booth when Lou arrived. After they placed their usual orders, Rosie described how Ted went right for the young woman with the great body.

"You know, Lou, I might not be hot stuff anymore, but I'm still stuff, and some of my stuff, though possibly lukewarm, is still pretty darn good. It may look like it's past its expiration date, but it's not, except maybe for the charming swinging of my upper arms."

They both laughed.

"It's hard to be a beginner in my fifties and feel like I'm doing something wrong, because I'm getting older. What's with that?"

Just then their food arrived, and the question would have to wait until another time. It's too easy to be distracted when Emberbergers with extra sauce and fries are placed in front of you.

* * *

For a short time after her Ted experience, Rosie went through a post-divorce-fairytale syndrome that she didn't expect. "Isn't a guy supposed to come and rescue me now? Where are you already?" She imagined his face, creating in her mind the perfect prince charming but quickly tossed that image out, knowing from experience that good looks are sometimes just a disguise. It would be cool, though, if he had that long coat that floated out behind him as he strode along, but that's negotiable. Not everyone can pull off a coat like that. How about a kind man? Ah, how underrated is that? And how would he rescue her?

He would love her.

Rosie remembered the boy she had seen at college during freshman orientation at the Davies Center Student Union. He was across the large room from her when their eyes connected, holding each other's for a brief moment. There were such possibilities in that connection. Then the crowd shifted, students began to leave, and he disappeared. Maybe she wasn't meant to find her soul mate this time around and wasn't quite sure what to think about that.

* * *

The next morning after chores, she collected the two client checks that had come in the mail the day before. For the past few weeks, she'd found herself humming melodies now and then, and driving to the bank to deposit her checks, she decided to sing.

"Aye, aye, yay, yay, my jeans are too tight and my crotch seam is really uncomfortable…aye, yay, yay, yay." It didn't take much for her to entertain herself.

That evening, Jill had gone out with a few of her teaching buddies, so Rosie had a quick dinner and went outside to sit on the porch. A light breeze kept away any hardy remaining mosquitoes.

She thought about Ron. She didn't believe he would change, though she believed there would always be opportunities for him to do so. She thought about the advice from Tom and John. By focusing on her healing, forgiveness was, indeed, slowly beginning to emerge from places where her pain had been. It was the pain that had saved her, that had woken her up when she could no longer tolerate it. So much of her had been chipped away over the years. She'd been picking up pieces of her life for quite a while and needed a break. Anything she missed, she'd find later. Rosie felt that the door that had closed all those years ago was opening once again but then wondered if there ever was a door. Only choices. She had chosen to face the truth about her marriage. The truths she'd believed about herself were changing, as well, but not without a fight, and she'd had some very interesting conversations with her fear and her anger and promised to listen to them and offer hugs whenever needed. As a result, they were all on pretty good terms. She thought of empty lilac bushes that would bloom again in the spring and watched as the sun slowly lowered itself into the horizon. She was no longer afraid of dark times. Well, maybe just a little, and that was fine.

Rosie had traveled beyond the boundaries of the life she had known, feeling as if she'd walked up treacherous hills and across rough stones, through soft meadows and gentle streams, and was now resting, surrounded by starlight and magic. Watching the sun leave streaks of marvelous colors as it ended its day, she decided, "I will paint this."